Anca's Story

a YA Holocaust novel

by

Saffina Desforges

ISBN-13: 978-1481283090

ISBN-10: 148128309X

Introduction.

The year 2015 will mark the 75th anniversary of the end of World War II. And with it, the 75th anniversary of the end of the event we call the Holocaust.

The last veterans of World War II have all but left us, and over the next two decades the last living souls old enough to have any memory of those events will pass on. World War II and the Holocaust will fade, literally, from living memory and become, in every sense of the word, history.

The characters in this story are fictional. The events we call the Holocaust were very, very real.

As the 75th anniversary of the liberation of Auschwitz approaches, we *shall* remember them.

Saffina Desforges

Chapter 1.

Replete in casual suit, no tie, and perfectly manicured nails, Mr. Wilkinson led me gently into the empty classroom.

Desks had been thoughtfully moved to one side, the seats arranged in rows in a semi-circle towards a single chair that I guessed it would be my privilege to occupy.

"Will this be comfortable enough for you?"

I nodded, easing forward on my walking frame, unable to speak.

My throat felt dry, my clammy hands held to my side to conceal the shake. I wanted to leave, to make my excuses and return to the security of my sheltered home, but fought against my instincts.

For weeks now I had been preparing for this day.

Making notes.

Drawing on long-forgotten memories.

Struggling to bring order to my thoughts.

Now, at last, the moment had arrived. The time had come, to relate a story I had kept buried deep within me for almost six decades. I prayed I could maintain my composure before my audience when they arrived.

My host seemed quite indifferent to my plight, chatting amiably about the curriculum. Only half-listening, I cast my eyes around the room, searching unsuccessfully for the comfort of a blackboard. My eyes alighted on a white screen. I caught my breath, interrupting Mr. Wilkinson to apologise for not having brought any slides along.

Mr. Wilkinson tried to hide a smile, explaining to me this was an interactive whiteboard.

My blank response saw him toying with a keyboard with practiced movements that put my own humble typing skills to shame, bringing the screen to life in a blaze of colour and sound. Maps and still photographs combined with video clips and commentary and suddenly I could witness the rise of Nazi Germany; Hitler's invasion of Poland; the Japanese attack on Pearl Harbour...

This was twenty-first century interactive education, Mr. Wilkinson explained with undisguised glee, extolling the virtues of IT in his class as if it were his personal invention.

Not just the Second World War, he stressed, but any other conflict I could care to mention, from the Mycenaean battles of antiquity to the more recent Gulf Wars. I need but name it and he could produce a file or web-site to bring it to life before my eyes.

I declined the offer, explaining that, for me, there was only one war.

His condescending smile said it all.

I was an old lady, living in the past, unable to see the greater picture.

And slowly I realised I had been invited here today not so much to bring recent history to life, but rather to say goodbye to it.

Chapter 2.

As I gathered my thoughts the door opened and the children began to file in. A few glanced my way and I responded with an awkward smile, unsure how best to acknowledge them.

I watched as they selected their positions in the semi-circle around me. One or two extracted notebooks and pens from their bags, but without much enthusiasm. Mostly they slumped into their seats and carried on their private discussions seemingly oblivious to my presence, as if hoping the lesson would be somehow delayed until they had finished.

"Settle down, 9B." The sharp rap of knuckles on wood brought the class to order.

With noisy sighs of resignation, they turned their attention to the teacher, some noticing me for the first time, staring at me. Perhaps wondering what sundry lecture I had been instructed to bore them with on this occasion.

"9B, that will do." Mr. Wilkinson's stern gaze dared them to dissent. After a few seconds he explained, "Today we have as our guest Mrs. Jones, who has kindly volunteered her time to talk to you about her personal experience of World War Two and the Holocaust. About how..."

I felt waves of panic sweep over me. I clutched my chair, closing my eyes, willing it to pass. For a moment I felt faint.

Mr. Wilkinson's words came back into focus. "...therefore I expect you all to give her your undivided attention for the next forty minutes and, hopefully, to come up with some..." He paused for effect. "Some intelligent questions to ask when she has finished."

There was a groan of dismay at this proposal and I realized few here wished to hear my story.

As I looked about me at these fresh young faces, thirteen and fourteen year olds whose idea of trauma was to miss a favourite television programme or to have their latest games console taken from them, I could see in their bright eyes a mirror of my own childhood, of my own indifference to even current affairs, let alone the past.

I remembered how irrelevant even the previous day's news had been. How could I possibly ask that these children be interested in what happened to me, seven decades ago, long before their parents were born? Perhaps even before their grandparents were born?

I studied their clean features, their shining hair, immaculately ironed clothes, polished shoes beneath socks neatly at half mast. In return they stared back, some sullenly, others in a spirit of hope over experience, waiting for me to start.

The sooner to finish, no doubt.

I chose my words carefully and began.

Chapter 3.

"My name is Anca. Anca Pasculata. Your teacher introduced me as Mrs. Jones, and that is indeed my name now, for I came to your country in nineteen forty-eight, married in nineteen fifty-four and have lived here in Great Britain ever since. But for today, for the purpose of this lesson, I am Anca Pasculata once more.

"The name is Romanian, for such are my origins. I was born in Romania and my parents, my family, were all of that country."

Blank faces stared back at me. I suspected they were as indifferent to geography as they were to history, and had no idea where Romania was.

No matter.

I gathered my thoughts. "I had thought to begin by explaining a little of the background to the war, but your teacher has shown me some of the remarkable materials you have to work with and I realise that is not necessary. To be honest, you probably know more about that even than I do."

I took a deep breath, conscious of the tremor in my voice

"So I shall begin not at the beginning but rather towards the end of the war, for that is when my own story starts. I want to take you back to a year before the war ended. To nineteen forty-four."

I paused to study my audience, already showing advanced signs of boredom. Someone stifled a yawn. Several were fidgeting with bags or equipment. One seemed to be texting from a mobile phone secreted behind their pencil-case. I pressed on, hoping somehow to earn their attention.

"I was twelve years old at this time. Just a little younger than you are now. I was lucky enough to have enjoyed an education until then, though it hardly compared with your own. School, for us, was a single, bare, unlit, un-heated classroom where paper and pencils were luxuries, and memory our most precious asset."

I was pleased to see a few heads turn my way. I pressed on.

"This was a time before computers, or even calculators. Before television, even in the advanced industrial countries like your own. For a backward, peasant country like Romania even radio and newspapers were luxuries beyond our day to day experience."

A couple of girls exchanged glances, perhaps trying to imagine life before computers.

I said, "Certainly I knew nothing of the world about me. Not even of the global nature of the war that had already been raging four long years by this time. Our country was under Nazi German domination, that much I knew. I vaguely understood other, neighbouring countries to be involved somehow, but to what end, on whose side, I neither knew nor cared. I was aware only of events in my own small world. And that world was one insignificant town in a backward, insular country in eastern Europe."

A boy to one side was whispering to his classmate. Mr. Wilkinson rapped a ruler on the desk.

"Ben, at least have the courtesy to be quiet, if you can't be bothered to listen. Mrs. Jones has been to a great deal of trouble to be here with us today."

The boy called Ben stretched out in his chair, a calculated show of disinterest. "Yeah, but it's boring, Sir. Why can't we do it on the computer instead, if we have to do it at all? No-one cares about history."

The boy cast his eyes about his fellow pupils conspiratorially before adding, "Least of all the Holocaust." The child looked directly at me. "It's only about dead Jews."

"One more remark like that and you'll be up before the Head." Mr. Wilkinson's sharp tone silenced the boy.

To me, "I'm so very sorry, Mrs Jones. Ben, you will apologise immediately."

Ben forced a sullen "Sorry, Miss," as he slunk back into his chair, privately delighted with his performance.

I smiled, addressing the boy directly. "I can assure you, Ben, that, if old and frail, I am still very much alive, and anticipate being around a few years more yet."

The class appreciated my little joke and I pushed home my advantage. "Nor, I might add, am I a Jew."

The teacher shot me a surprised look.

I said, "Mr Wilkinson asked me to bring along any personal effects I had, to help illustrate my story. Photographs of my family and friends; mementoes of that time. Of the Holocaust." I splayed my empty hands theatrically. "You will notice I have brought nothing."

I felt the eyes of the class on my empty hands. "I brought nothing because I have nothing. Everything, every possession I had, was destroyed or left behind. Not a single token or memento survived with me."

If the words brought a lump to my own throat still there was indifference from my audience and I knew that, if I did not soon capture their minds I would never move their hearts. I asked, "Tell me this. How many of you have lost a parent?"

There was a stunned silence. Two hands rose awkwardly.

"Forgive my intrusion, but what happened to them?"

Mr. Wilkinson cast an anxious glance at me, but I ignored his concerns, directing my attention to the two children whose hands hovered hesitantly above their heads.

"My mother was killed in a car accident, a few years ago."

"I am sorry. So very sorry." I turned to the second child, a boy. "And you?"

"Cancer. My father died of cancer, soon after I was born. I never knew him."

The class shifted uncomfortably in their seats. Mr Wilkinson looked on, unsure how to respond. This was not what I had been invited to discuss.

I said, "Thank you. You are brave to talk about it. But I asked with good reason, to make a point. Most of you have two parents. Two of you have lost one. I lost my father when I was twelve years old. But not to cancer. Not to a car accident."

I paused, struggling to control the quaver in my voice. "He was murdered. Murdered in cold blood, by a firing squad outside our home, while my mother, my younger brother and I were forced to watch."

I had their attention now, this class of bright-eyed children that had no acquaintance with evil. I chose my words carefully.

"History states the war began in nineteen thirty-nine, when Germany invaded Poland. Perhaps it was so. But for me the war began with my father's death.

"My story begins as the war entered its final year, just a few weeks after my father's execution. In a storm-swept cemetery in Medgidia, Romania, in the early spring of nineteen forty-four..."

Chapter 4.

We stood in silent reverence, my mother and I, before the pitiful mound that marked my father's grave. Driving rain lashed the sodden black earth, each drop drawing another grain of soil into the murky pools that formed unbidden at its base.

At the head of the grave a crudely shaped rowan cross defied the elements, proud against the rolling clouds that had advanced afternoon into premature evening. A flash of lightning briefly cast shadows as it lit the sky, to be greeted by thunderous applause.

I clasped my mother's hand tightly, fighting a losing battle to hold back tears that joined with the rain to trace the contours of my face. Instinctively I ran my tongue over my lips, the salt stimulating my taste buds, conjuring welcome, evocative memories.

The Black Sea, near Constanta. Salt spray lingering in the air as the spring wind flung the waves against the foreshore, the surf frothing, foaming, against the beach. Nearly two years had since passed, but the memories were as if it were yesterday. It had been soon after my tenth birthday. The spring of nineteen forty-two. A special holiday for his little nurse, as Papa always called me. To recuperate from some malady long since over.

"Papa, I will never forget you," I said beneath my breath. "Never."

My mother glanced at me. "Anca?"

"It was nothing, Mama. Just thinking out loud. But we should be going now, for Nicolae is tired. You surely must be, too."

To reply, to acknowledge my assertion, was pointless. Words were cumbersome, even unnecessary at times like this. A clash of thunder drowned out any reply she may have made.

"The storm is receding," I observed quietly as we turned a corner and found ourselves on the main road, a short distance from our home.

"It is as well, Anca," my mother concurred. "You and Nicolae will sleep better for it. There is enough noise through the night without nature adding her own."

I smiled agreement. These past few weeks I had hardly slept of a night, kept awake by the constant drone of passing trucks and tanks.

Behind us a vehicle's throbbing engine spewed unseen exhaust fumes into the early night. Heads down, our eyes scanned the truck as it passed. In the tenebrous dusk their uniforms were unclear. Not that it mattered anymore. Iron Guard or Gestapo, Papa had said they were of the same breed. Whatever their nationality. Whatever their chosen name.

Only when the truck had passed into the darkness did we breathe again.

The rain had begun to ease now and by the time we reached home it had reduced to a fine drizzle, but still the smell of wet hair and sodden clothes quickly permeated every corner of our small domicile.

Nicolae, by now asleep, was laid to rest on a threadbare rug. I gently towelled his hair with a dry cloth while Mama brought a thin counterpane to lay over him. Fortunately, Mama's coat had borne the brunt of the storm's attack and Nicolae's clothes were still dry. I slipped shoes from his tiny feet and made him comfortable as best I could, gently stroking his rouge cheek, a smile hovering on my own lips in the certain knowledge he, at least, was resting peacefully.

Chapter 5.

Mama forewent the pleasure of dry clothing and made immediately for the parlour to prepare a simple repast. Only once Nicolae and I were fed and in our beds would Mama tend her own needs.

With some effort I braved the discomfort and declined to change my own clothes, beyond removing my thin, inadequate coat.

An oil-burning lamp held the darkness at bay while I fostered a small wood fire in the grate. As the flames gained confidence the room slowly brightened and I turned out the lamp, conscious that fuel was precious and we knew not when more might be available.

When the meal was ready Nicolae was gently awoken and we sat cross-legged around the fire, enjoying the warmth, drawing comfort from lambent flames that cast flickering shadows around the sparsely furnished room.

For a while the dull clatter of wooden spoons against clay provided the only accompaniment as cutlery chased food to hungry mouths. It was a meagre offering of a bland maize-based gruel, enhanced by a few welcome slivers of mutton which Mama had somehow acquired. But we were grateful now for what we would have viewed with contempt just months before.

Papa had been provident to our needs, but upon his arrest all but our most basic goods and chattels were seized by the Nazis, and after Papa's execution we were overnight reduced to a state of indigence, without an income or pension of any sort.

Somehow, Mama obtained the odd bani to keep us fed, though whenever I tried to enquire how she would become agitated and instigate a discussion of some other matter.

Nicolae, too tired to talk, and warmed by the fire, fell asleep again even before he had consumed what little food had been made available for him.

Despite my token objections, Mama poured the remainder into my bowl, from where it quickly disappeared.

While Mama carried Nicolae to bed I took the empty bowls and rinsed the earthenware in a pail of rain water reserved for the purpose. Clean water was as precious a commodity as food and fuel now, and we used it sparingly.

At last it was time to sleep and I gratefully relinquished my wet clothes to Mama, who draped them as best she could before the dwindling fire in the hope they might be dry by morning.

It had been a long day and for once, my constitution fortified by the warm meal, I was able to join Nicolae in slumber with fewer than usual of the hours of tossing and turning that had marked my recent bedtimes.

Chapter 6.

I next opened my eyes to a flood of sunlight through the broken window pane. Dust sparkled as it floated timelessly above me, ensnared in a rectangle of light that slew through the gloom of my chamber to play casually upon the splintered wooden floor.

Through the jagged shards of glass the branches of an olive tree diluted the sun's glare as she forged her way above the horizon, a few defiant clouds daring to challenge the welcome orb that announced the arrival of each new day. I reached out a hand into the beam of light, enjoying the warmth against my skin, the dust swirling anxiously around my extended limb, as if trapped by some invisible border.

Outside, the dawn chorus was already underway, a welcome aubade to the new day, for the social and political upheavals of recent times seemed to have had no impact on the fauna around us.

I could hear Mama as she went about her chores, determined our abode should be respectable at the beginning of each day, cleaning and clearing what it had been too dark to tend the previous evening.

A smile crept across my lips, broadening as I became conscious of it. Happiness was not a commodity in great supply at this time and I welcomed it with open heart. Perhaps it was a sign that things were to change for the better.

I rose quietly and washed from a bowl of water prepared the night before. For nearly a year now we had been obliged to follow this cumbersome routine, to allow to settle the sediment that spewed forth from the communal faucet a few roads distant.

Nicolae slept undisturbed through my ablutions, as I wished. We had always shared a room, since before I can remember, but I had reached that age now where privacy was beginning to assume increasing importance.

This was a difficult time for me. I was aware of the changes taking place within my body, yet unable to fully understand them. There was no-one of whom I could seek explanation, for Mama still thought of me as a little child.

And now... Now I found myself without a mentor in the form of teacher or friend, in whom I could confide.

Mama was still busy with her chores and after exchanging perfunctory salutations, I passed through to the garden, to view the church clock on which we all relied for our time-keeping. It was a symbol of our village, defiant of the coming and going of those below. A sign of security and continuity in moments of national crisis.

As with King Carol's abdication. We, the entire village, I should not be surprised, had stood, studying the hands of the time-piece, in order to bow our heads in reverence on the hour of his son's succession.

All but Papa, whose contempt for the new King Michael lost him many friends. I'd heard it whispered this had been a pertinent factor in his arrest. As much so as the workers' strike in the Ploesti oil fields. But as yet, the political machinations of the adult world were quite beyond my understanding.

For me, the clock was my guide to attending school.

Papa had always been insistent that my schooling was of the utmost importance. And so few children were able to benefit from an education, least of all girls, that I ought perhaps to have felt privileged.

But even when Papa were alive I had gained no enjoyment from my scholarship, surrounded by peers who seemed to look down on me because of my background. Because my father was of the labouring classes, a humble engineer of the oil industry, not part of the intelligentsia.

Despite this I had made a few friends, and my preceptor had, at first, given me encouragement and helped me to learn.

But then, after the workers' strike, when Papa was arrested, everything changed.

Chapter 7.

Mama had insisted I continue to attend class, despite my protests. She said Papa would have wished it so. That it was for my future. That I would have to support Nicolae if anything happened to her.

And of course, she was entirely right. It is a peculiar feature of childhood that, the less years you have behind you, the more difficult to plan for that which is still to come. But at the time I could not help thinking she just wanted me out of the house.

This was a belief that had been reinforced just days previously, when I had been sent home from school early, heavy with sickness.

I had entered the house to find Mama in the company of a uniformed soldier. I was stricken with panic, fearing he had come to remove her as they had Papa. But fear turned to wild incomprehension as realization dawned he was there as her guest, made welcome in our very home, his jacket draped over a chair, his boots at the door.

After all she had said of them.

After what they had done to Papa.

I had run to my room, flinging the door shut, overwhelmed with tears.

Tears of confusion.

Of frustration.

Of betrayal.

My thoughts were myriad and it took some while for Mama to comfort me to a state where I could converse rationally.

Through her own tears she had tried to justify herself. He was Romanian, like us, she had said. Not a German. An officer of the Iron Guard, not of the Gestapo.

As if this somehow lessened the crime.

But when I demanded to know the precise nature of her entertainment she screamed incoherently at me and ran to the privacy of her room, shouting that the welfare of her children had to come before all else.

Of course, I was too young then to appreciate her sacrifice.

The bell began tolling its notice of time's passing, intruding the present into my thoughts once more, and I realized I would be late. I hurried myself to the road, shouting a final farewell to Mama as I left.

Chapter 8.

I learned of the resettlement plans when I arrived home that evening.

It had not been an easy day for me. There were no easy days any more.

My teacher, whom once I might have confided in, now treated me as if I had personally wronged her.

My friends – as I once considered them, and as I tried, desperately, still to do – were also distant, my family ostracised.

They made no accusation. How could they? I had done nothing.

But from the day of Papa's arrest their attitudes had changed.

I received no explanation.

Nor, in truth, could I expect one.

Their stance was not new to me. Only their target.

I was not a gypsy. Nor a Jew. Nor even a Slav.

My crime... My crime was that of my father. Dear Papa.

I reached our door, pushing against the splintered wood. Rusting hinges announced their objection. I peered into the gloom, stepping over the threshold, pausing while my eyes adjusted to the light.

"Anca?"

"Mama."

I perceived my mother, seated on a wooden stool by the unlit fire. Nicolae lay asleep on the floor beside her, a sackcloth providing a little warmth on this cool spring evening. I rushed to hug my mother and we embraced as though our parting had been of weeks, months, not the few hours that had passed for day.

The ensuing silence warned me all was not well. I relaxed my hold, looking into her eyes, searching for a clue.

I could see she had been crying, and felt tears moisten my own eyes in empathy, but I fought them back, conscious of some vague sense of responsibility.

"What is it, Mama? What has happened?"

My mother clutched me gently to her breast. I felt her chest rise as she took a deep breath while she composed her response. The words, when they finally came, were not unexpected, but no less unwelcome for that.

"We are to move, Anca."

I remained motionless, allowing the news to sink slowly into my mind. Mama turned away, unable to meet my gaze.

After Papa's execution we were told we might be moved to another town. To ease the ill-feeling, they had told us. The officer had seemed a kindly man, soft spoken, his concern for our welfare apparently sincere. Yet he wore the uniform of those who had killed Papa. How could we trust him? Believe him?

"Where to?"

I asked the question only to break the silence. The destination was of no importance, the reply unfamiliar and instantly forgotten. I had already prepared a more relevant question.

"When are we to leave, Mama?"

"Tomorrow. Noon."

The answer stunned me. "Tomorrow? But..."

My words faded as I realised my objections were unsound. We had so little to pack. Such belongings that had not been punitively seized by the Nazis had been quickly sold. Our furnishings – those which we had not bartered for food – had been broken up to keep a fire at night for Nicolae. Our clothes were few beyond those we now wore. And now we... I... Had no friends even to bid goodbye. I became conscious that Mama was speaking again.

"First we must go to Bucharest. There we will be given further directions. We must be at the station before noon, Anca."

The station. Memories flooded by mind. I was on the train. Constanta. The hiss of steam. The lurch forward as the wheels struggled for grip. I was eleven. My first ever journey by train.

"Are we going somewhere, Mama?"

Nicolae had awoken. My thoughts jolted back to reality. The present. Cold reality.

Nicolae's eyes shone bright with curiosity, as if he had been awake all the time. Perhaps he had not slept. It was not easy to sleep anymore. I could shut my eyes, but events would not allow rest. They followed even into my dreams.

Perhaps Nicolae shared the same experiences, I did not know. He was only six. Soon to be seven. I was not even sure when.

Time meant little to me. To anyone.

An unknown future.

A present ridden by fear.

Only the past held happiness.

Certainty.

Nicolae's little fingers clutched my own. His face came into focus, his eyes on mine.

"Anca?"

Mama had moved to the parlour, preparing a meal. I realized Nicolae was looking to me for the answer. I had none to offer.

"Rest, little one. It is late." I took his hand, offering a smile and the reassurance of a firm grip. He smiled back, gripping my hand tight. That special bond between brother and sister.

Mama shortly brought our meal to us and we consumed it with grateful thanks. Long past was the time when we might pick and choose from the bowl, leaving anything that had no appeal. Now every morsel was relished, for we never knew how long might pass before the next.

As we scraped our platters clean, Mama said, "Dear Nicolae, please try to sleep now. We have a busy day tomorrow."

I echoed her sentiments, pulling my brother's frail body to my own, hugging him, savouring him. My other hand stretched to meet Mama's, but I could not bring myself to look into her eyes. Instead I turned again to my sibling.

"Tomorrow, Nicolae, Mama and I are taking you on a special journey. On the train."

"The train?" Nicolae's face broke into a smile. "Oh, Mama, can I sit closest to the window? Please, Mama? I will be good! Are we going to the seaside? Anca, where is it we are going?" His voice bubbled with the excitement that only small children, unburdened by life's harsh reality, can extol. I found myself wishing I too was six years old again.

"Hush, little one, hush," I reproached him. "Our destination is a surprise for you and me both. Only Mama knows where we are bound. But you must rest now, or you will be too tired in the morning to enjoy yourself."

"We must all rest now, Anca. You too," Mama urged. "Tomorrow will be a tiring day, of that I am quite certain." I felt her grip on my hand strengthen before reluctantly letting go. She gestured to Nicolae. "Anca, would you? My back troubles me tonight." She bent over Nicolae and kissed him gently.

"Good night, Nicolae. God bless you."

"Good night, Mama. Please let us go to the seaside tomorrow."

I stood up, lifting Nicolae, stooping to kiss Mama. Our eyes met. "Good night, Mama. I love you."

She tried to reply but the words would not come. Myriad emotions swam in her eyes. Then, at last, "God bless, Anca."

I carried Nicolae through to our room and lay him prostrate on his bunk.

"Do you think we will be going to the seaside, Anca?" he demanded, as I pulled his shoes from his feet.

"I cannot say, Nicolae. Only that if you do not sleep soon then Mama may change her mind and we will go nowhere at all."

A startled expression crossed his face. "I am asleep, Anca. Look!" He held his eyes tightly shut, simulating slumber, fighting to restrain a smile.

"Good night, little one." I kissed his forehead before crossing to my own bed, slowly undressing, hesitantly slipping beneath the cover.

Across the room Nicolae's breathing eased as act became reality and sleep took its inevitable hold. I was not to be so fortunate, shifting restlessly through the evening, feigning sleep when Mama pushed open the door to check on us.

Eventually I must have dozed, for I awoke some while later to the sound of crying. At first I thought it was Nicolae, but as my mind cleared itself of a cobweb of dreams I realised the sound came from Mama's room.

I quietly rose and crossed to the door to offer comfort, but seeing her at the table, gently sobbing before a tiny candle which desperately parried the encroaching night, I hesitated. She had a quill in her hand and was, I presumed, attending her diary, for I knew she kept one.

I paused at the doorway a while, before returning to my bed unannounced. Sometimes it was best to be left alone, I knew. Mama believed us both to be in slumber and so it would remain. I slipped once again beneath my covers and cried myself gently to sleep.

Chapter 9.

Morning crept quietly upon us, the dawn's advancing light filtering through the window, inexorably consuming the night's shadows as no candle could ever do. Across the room Nicolae still slept.

Throwing back the covers I allowed my body to bask in the warm sunshine. Two days now of fair weather, I reminded myself. Perhaps the pattern of inclemency that had distinguished the past weeks had finally been broken. Many times recently I had awoken shivering in the cool March air, hurrying to dress. Yet today it were as if summer were upon us.

For a few seconds I allowed memories of summers past to procreate in my mind, but they were banished by a clatter of activity from the parlour, bringing me back to the present. Mama would need help to prepare for our journey.

Climbing from my bed I paused in the stream of dilute sunlight, stretching my body taut until the muscles in my back and legs surrendered to the strain and relaxed, leaving me limber and ready for whatever the day might bring. The splash of cold water from the basin in a still dark corner of the room provided the final incentive my body needed to cast off the dreariness residual from the night's sleep.

Today, able to return to the sun's warmth to dry, the morning wash was a welcome start to the day. Through the long winter months ablutions had not been so pleasant, on many occasions it being necessary to break ice from the basin first. My body shivered at the memory.

I turned to see Nicolae had awoken and lay quietly in his bed, watching me. He face bore the innocent smile of a carefree child.

I donned a hessian smock and slipped my feet into a pair of calf-skin shoes, now badly in need of repair. They had been a present for my eleventh birthday. Then I had been the envy of my school-friends, and I smiled to think of how they clamoured to be allowed to try them on themselves.

Such fond memories.

But only memories.

Now, already twelve, my feet had grown such that the calf-skin was stretched to its limit, discomfort a constant feature of their wear, but complaint was pointless, for they were all I had.

"Is that Mama?" Nicolae asked.

I became aware of my mother singing quietly to herself as she went about her business. As I listened a smile parted my lips. It was a welcome note of cheer which, abetted by the warm sunshine that irradiated our room, lifted my heart.

"Arise now, little one," I beckoned. "Mama will need help to get ready. Today we are to embark upon a new adventure."

Chapter 10.

I found Mama carefully packing our belongings into a small wooden trunk.

"Anca, good morning, dearest." We embraced. "You slept well?"

"Thank you, Mama, yes." I had not, but saw no value in relating this fact.

"And Nicolae?"

I could answer more truthfully this time, so was more liberal with my response. "He slept very well, Mama. He has just awoken and is even now dressing in anticipation of our journey. He is so excited, Mama! Really, you should see his smile!"

Mama's face beamed.

"And you, Mama? You have rested, I trust? You seem so cheerful this morning." I did not relate I had seen her upset the previous night, but hoped she might allude to it, that I might ask further. But in this I was to be disappointed.

"We have had time enough to dwell on the past, Anca. Now we must embrace the future. Thus am I engaged, as you see."

"Permit me help you, Mama."

She forced a laugh, gesturing to the half-full case. "That is hardly necessary, my child."

A single glance assured me she was correct in her assertion, for almost everything we owned was now packed in readiness for our departure.

"Besides," I heard her continue, "I have a special task for you."

"Mama?"

"I want you to take Nicolae and go for a walk this morning."

"A walk?" This was an unexpected request. I knew we had no money to spare, and the local vendors had long since ceased to provide us with credit.

"Around the town, Anca. To say goodbye, to your friends... To the town in which you were born." Mama's smile faded and her voice became choked.

She took my hand. "Perhaps to Papa's grave, a final time? Anca, please understand, in all probability we will never return to Medgidia. At the very least, not before this evil war is over."

She gestured once more to the trunk. "All our worldly possessions will be with us in this one valise, Anca. But far more important are our memories, of happier times, for nothing and no-one can take those from us. Please, Anca, do as I ask. Take Nicolae with you and savour your home town a final time."

I watched a tear roll down her cheek and knew protest was pointless.

Of course I must pay a final visit to Papa's grave. Yet I could not bring myself to seek out friends as Mama suggested, for they had, with one exception, all turned against me. But then I thought of Raisa, and knew Mama was right. If even that friendship had soured recently, it was through events beyond control of either of us. It was wrong of me to hold Raisa responsible for her parents' judgements.

"You will join us, of course?" It was a rhetorical question, for it was inconceivable that Mama would not wish to visit Papa's grave a final time herself. Her answer was therefore all the more surprising.

"No, Anca, I must remain here."

"But Mama, why?"

She hesitated briefly, as if unsure herself, then, "Our travel documents are to be delivered this morning."

My surprised expression demanded further explanation.

"An officer came last night," Mama said. "He will be calling this morning to bring them."

"Last night? But..." My voice trailed. I had no recollection of such a visitor. It was not possible anyone had attended and I not be aware of the fact.

"After you had gone to bed, Anca. Very late." Mama's voice quavered and she fought to control it. "You were asleep, my child."

My eyes searched hers and she looked away. I could only conclude there had been no visitors. But why would Mama fabricate such a story?

Confused, perhaps feeling betrayed, I let Mama continue with her fiction. All would be explained eventually, I was certain, and my mother would surely stand justified in her actions.

Chapter 11.

At that moment Nicolae appeared in the doorway, his smiling face beaming at us. "Is it time to go on the train yet?"

Mama seized upon the interruption, turning to embrace her son, and I let the matter pass. Soon afterwards, having said an emotional farewell to Papa at the cemetery, Nicolae and I were walking hand in hand around Medgidia. While my little brother babbled excitedly about the pending train journey I looked about me with keen eyes, trying to convert to memory the scenes that for all my life I had taken for granted.

Suddenly the town had assumed a new appeal, for all the ravages of recent decline, and I felt disconsolate to be leaving. As we approached Raisa's home I became more despondent still. Where once I had had so many friends, now only Raisa stood worthy of the name. I consoled myself with the thought that, if friendships were so easily broken, perhaps they had not been true friends at all.

But Raisa was more than just a friend. She was my best friend, and I knew that meant I must risk the wrath of her parents to see her one final time.

As we arrived outside her home the prospect was indeed daunting. Our companionship had been forbidden after Papa's arrest and we had since met only infrequently, clandestinely, after school. Now I paused at her door, hand poised, not quite able to muster the confidence to knock.

"Anca, come on! Knock on the door!" It was Nicolae, with child-like impatience, blissfully ignorant of my dilemma. He reached up, standing on tip-toe, and clasped the brass knocker in his tiny hand, rapping it against the plate. The deed was done.

"Thank you, Nicolae. Thank you."

While my brother skipped about the path I stood in sombre silence, dreading the confrontation. How to explain to Raisa's parents? That I would never see my best friend, their daughter, again. What did such childhood friendships mean to adults? They were as nothing.

I prayed her mother would attend, thinking I could argue my case more easily with a woman than a man, but before I could decide upon a strategy the door opened and Raisa's father, Maxim, stood before us.

For a moment I stood in awed silence, unable to mouth my wishes. He stared back, clearly stunned by my temerity, that I would defy his authority so brazenly as to attend his doorstep in broad daylight after what had happened.

"Anca?"

"Please, I must see Raisa."

He stood across the doorway, his posture confirming his words. "I believe I asked you not to come here, child."

My eyes filled with tears and I reached out an imploring hand. "Please, just this once. We are leaving today. Forever. I must say goodbye to Raisa."

Obdurate to my lachrymose appeal, my friend's father responded with a silent shake of his head and began to step back inside, his hand on the door to close it. "Go, Anca. You are no longer welcome here."

"No! Please, no!" Tears flooded my cheeks as reality dawned, that I would never see Raisa again. "I have to say goodbye. Raisa is my best friend... My only friend."

My words must have had some impact, for Maxim hesitated, then stepped forward and looked up and down the street. He turned to me again, and pushed the door open. "She is in the back room. Go quickly, and bid your farewell, child. Then be gone."

Chapter 12.

I needed no further encouragement.

I knew my way about the house from many visits in halcyon days past and hurried through, aware Nicolae was being beckoned into the house behind me, to avoid drawing unwanted attention by remaining at the door.

If Raisa's home had fared better than our own, still there were signs that recent events had taken their toll. Much furniture had gone, presumably sold to make ends meet, and I knew that, if times had been hard for everyone, it was especially difficult for Raisa's family.

They were Russian immigrants. Refugees from our giant neighbour during the upheavals there. It was strange now to think that it was Papa that had made them welcome in Medgidia when first they arrived, without a home or work, barely able to speak our language. Thus it was that I had first met Raisa. We had been friends now for so many years I could hardly remember a time when we did not know one another.

I pushed the door open and saw Raisa at the table, sewing. She looked up in surprise as she saw me, then leapt to greet me, at once delighted and confused, for it had been an indeterminable time since I had been allowed to visit her. Her father had forbidden any contact between us after Papa's execution, yet now here I was in her own home once more.

"Anca! Anca! What are you doing here? If Papa finds you he will—"

Raisa's father appeared in the doorway. "It is okay, Raisa. I invited Anca in. I am given to understand she will be leaving today. This will be the last time you will see her. That is correct, Anca?"

I nodded, almost as confused as Raisa by her father's sudden change of heart. "We are to be at the station at noon."

"The station? But Anca, where? Who else is going? What will become of you?" Raisa choked out the questions as if fearing her father would rescind his decision before she could complete her enquiries.

As she spoke she moved across to me and we embraced as the friends we had always been. She began to cry, and I knew I could not long control my own emotions.

"Nicolae, come through with me, child," I heard her father say. "Let us give these girls some privacy."

I watched over Raisa's shoulder as her father led Nicolae away, pulling the door closed. For a moment we leaned against one another, savouring the physical contact, then I clasped Raisa's shoulders and pushed her to arms length, studying her face.

She implored me, "Anca, tell me it is not true. You are really leaving?"

"It is so, Raisa. Mama, Nicolae and I... It is for the best."

"But where? Where are you bound?"

I shook my head. "I forget the name. It is a resettlement camp of some sort. We will be given a place to live, to work, until the war is over. Far from here, I know that much, for we are to travel by train. And then..."

I looked deep into her eyes as words failed me. "And then, I do not know. But it cannot be worse than staying here in Medgidia. There is nothing left here for us, Raisa, please understand that. You are the only friend I have left, and I am forbidden to see even you."

"But Papa let you in this day, Anca. Perhaps he has had a change of heart?" Her eyes shone with hope.

"To avoid a scene at the door, Raisa, nothing more. That and to allow his daughter a final farewell to her friend."

Raisa embraced me again, saying, "No, Anca, not final. We will meet again, sometime in the future, when the war is over. I promise you we will. One day it will end, and people will live together peacefully once more. It must end, Anca, for otherwise what point is there to life? Wherever you go, whatever happens, promise you will remember me. Remember the good times we enjoyed together."

I clutched her to my breast and we cried together, as only best friends can.

I recall once Papa asking me what it was that distinguished a friend from a best friend. I answered that, in the company of a best friend, there was no need to act. One could be true to oneself and not fear to lose that friendship.

I knew now, as we held each other close, that Raisa was and would always be my one best friend.

As we cried together, without embarrassment or shame, I savoured her presence, as she mine. And as the tears expired we began to talk, one to the other in desultory fashion, speaking meaningless phrases, asking questions that had no answers, relating stories that had no point, enjoying the very act of communication as only children our age could.

Chapter 13.

At length the door pushed ajar and Raisa's father made his presence known with a discreet knock. We had by now exhausted our emotional distress and were smiling and laughing once more.

"Anca, I must ask that you leave us now." He added, "Please."

"I understand." I turned to Raisa once more and we embraced a final time, hugging each other tightly.

"Remember me always, Anca," she said. She retrieved a chain and amulet from around her neck and placed it over my head. I had never known her remove it before. "Promise me you will wear this always, Anca, so that you will always have me near your heart."

"But Raisa, I cannot..."

"You must, Anca. You can return it to me when next we see each other. Isn't that right, Papa?"

I turned to her father, seeking permission to accept this gift of friendship. He nodded his reluctant assent.

"I will treasure it always."

"I will immediately demand to see it when next we meet, Anca, no matter how many years may pass between."

"It will never leave my person. I promise, Raisa."

"You will write?"

"If at all possible."

"Goodbye then, Anca. Dearest friend."

"Farewell, Raisa."

We exchanged a final embrace and I followed Raisa's father from the room. I turned in the doorway to offer a final wave as he drew the door to behind me. Raisa wiped away a tear as she waved back. The door closed and I knew we would never see one another again.

"Anca." Raisa's father, Maxim, paused at the main door. "I want you to know how sorry I am, that it should end this way."

I looked up at him. Lugubrious features returned my gaze.

"It was not my wish to separate you two," Maxim said quietly. "I treasure my daughter, and value her friends. You, Anca, more than any other, for you must know how close your father and I were, before..."

He took my hand. "You are much too young to understand, Anca, but please believe me when I tell you that my actions were for the best. To allow your friendship with Raisa to continue after what happened to your father would have been foolhardy, benefiting neither party."

I looked into his eyes, trying to understand, wanting to believe his actions were well-intentioned, but unable to make sense of his reasons.

"Before we moved to your country we suffered persecution in our own homeland, Anca. We have seen it happen before. Please understand that I terminated your friendship with my daughter to protect her, not to grieve her."

I knew not how to respond, so I just listened.

"You are a wonderful child, Anca, and deserve so much better than the cruel hand fate has dealt you. But we cannot change things. Only sit quietly to one side and hope the worst will pass us by." He clasped my hand tightly, staring earnestly into my eyes.

"That was the mistake your father made, Anca. He was a brave man, but bravery means nothing to these barbarians. Your father was a hero. You can be proud of him."

He had my full attention now.

"But he paid the price. It was a salutary lesson to us all, Anca. One day you will understand, that I have acted only in Raisa's best interests. To put her safety before her childhood friendship. Please forgive me, Anca, as I hope Raisa will do one day. Now go. Good luck with whatever the future may bring. Wherever you may go, be assured Raisa will remember you." His long fingers took the amulet around my neck and tucked it gently inside my coat. He forced a smile. "Be sure to return this when next you see her."

If it was a difficult speech for me to take in, how much harder for this man to make it. I saw tears well in his dark eyes and knew every word was heartfelt. He was frightened. Frightened for his family, for his wife Catherine, and for his only daughter.

Just an hour earlier I had been filled with hatred for this man, who had dared come between me and my friend. Now I felt only sympathy.

As I clutched his hand I stretched up and kissed him on the cheek. "I am trying to understand, Maxim. I am trying so hard. Please, let no harm come to Raisa. My heart will always be with her." I turned and, taking Nicolae by the arm, walked into the street without a backward glance.

The journey home was slow and sombre. Nicolae was by now tiring, entreating me to carry him, but I was in no mood for such activity, my thoughts elsewhere. As we arrived at our own home I stopped outside, ushering Nicolae through.

"You go on ahead, Nicolae. I will join you shortly."

Nicolae looked up at me. "Why are you crying, Anca?"

I struggled to maintain my composure. "I have a speck of dust in my eye, little one, that is all. Now go on in and see if Mama needs any help to pack. It must be nearly time for the train."

At this reminder Nicolae sped off into the house, leaving me alone with my thoughts and once more the tears flowed.

Chapter 14.

We arrived at the station in good time for our departure. The fine weather had succumbed to cloud as the morning progressed and by noon the sky hung menacingly low, a tapestry of hysterical grays that forebode storms to come. Already the wind was beginning to strengthen, callously swirling dust before us and I found myself longing for rain to dampen the ground once more. In this, at least, I was not to be disappointed.

On arrival Mama took receipt of the travel documents from the station master's office. I briefly considered challenging her earlier story, that they were to have been delivered to our home that morning, but decided against it. From recent experience I knew such queries would only cause friction between us.

I glanced at the papers as they exchanged hands, but they were written in German and meant nothing to me. The station master made clear we must first take the train to Bucharest, our once proud capital.

I lay our trunk on the ground beside the rail track to form a seat for Mama, but she preferred to stand, so I sat down with Nicolae to try and occupy him. This one valise contained all our worldly belongings beyond the clothes we wore. All that we possessed of our past, to see us into the unknown future. It was a sobering thought, for I remembered how we had taken three such trunks on our holiday to Constanta for what had only been a few days away from home.

But these melancholy deliberations were quickly dismissed as Nicolae's excited cries brought my mind back into focus. Keen eyes and ears, undimmed by events that had dulled the senses of his elders, had identified a flume of steam in the distance and, even above the developing storm, the unmistakable sound of an approaching locomotive.

"Do not allow yourself to become too excited, Nicolae," I cautioned him gently. "It may not be the train we are waiting for."

"But it is, Anca. I know it is." My brother was determined in his supposition. His voice bubbled excitedly, "Look! Can you see it! Mama, I can see the smoke!"

"Steam, Nicolae, steam," I corrected him, almost without thinking. It was an unimportant point, but Papa always said that lax use of language was the sign of an indolent mind. As with so many things Papa had told me, his words somehow assumed new significance once he was gone.

By now, to my brother's delight, the locomotive was upon us, screeching wheels and hissing steam deafening as the engine passed us by, trailed by a snake of grime-ridden carriages until, at last, the cumbersome procession shuddered to a noisy, grinding halt. Little Nicolae was utterly enthralled by the sight, his eyes wide, his mouth open, desperately trying to count the carriages that passed us.

As the steam dissipated the carriages suddenly burst into activity, doors opening and slamming shut, people mounting or disembarking according to their need. I felt Mama tugging my arm, urging me to follow her.

Grabbing our trunk and pushing Nicolae before me, I hurried to match Mama's steps as she made her way to the most distant part of the train and opened the door for us to board. I heaved our case onto the step, lifting Nicolae on behind it, urging him to quickly find a seat.

The only other passengers this far back were a family of Jews, instantly identified as such by the yellow star they were obliged to wear sewn to their clothes. They huddled together in the far end of the carriage from us, studying our embarkation with suspicious eyes.

Mama appeared not to notice them, or if she did she gave no indication, and directed us to the far end of the carriage where she elected to sit with her back to her fellow travellers. Nicolae and I sat opposite her, by chance affording ourselves a clear view of the huddled family, although out of politeness I tried to appear disinterested.

Chapter 15.

Barely had we settled into our seats than a loud whistle shrilled and the train lurched forwards, the locomotive's wheels screaming, desperate for traction against the wet rails. Then suddenly we were moving, the carriage adopting a gentle sway as we gathered speed.

At first the steam from the engine threatened to engulf us, but as our momentum increased the steam was whipped away by the wind and through the rain-spattered windows we were able to slowly watch Medgidia disappear from sight, forever.

I felt afraid.

Alone and afraid.

I leaned over and took Mama's hand, the action serving to distract her from deeper considerations. Her eyes focused on me and she smiled. Her fingers clutched mine.

As if reading my thoughts, she said, "A new beginning, Anca. A fresh start. It will not be easy, my precious, but if we stick together, and have faith in the Almighty, everything will be all right, you will see."

I relaxed, warmed by these sentiments, as sanguine as any I had heard expressed in recent months. Of course we could not know the future, but we had every reason to be hopeful. It would, after all, be difficult to find ourselves in circumstances more dire than those we had just left behind.

I sat quietly, watching the changing scenery through the window.

"Nicolae, don't stare so. Have I brought you up so badly?" It was Mama, cautioning my little brother for his curiosity. Fascinated by the garb and style of our fellow passengers, Nicolae had been watching them intently, making occasional eye-contact with a child, a girl of perhaps eight or nine, that formed the youngest member of their party.

Nicolae shuffled uncomfortably in his seat at Mama's admonishment and stared sullenly out of the window.

My attention too had been directed at the family, although for different reasons. Through chance rather than design, our family had never occasioned acquaintance with the few Jews in Medgidia, and for me it was an opportunity to try and see what it was about these people that invited the ridicule and abuse they seemed so readily to attract.

But such an analysis seemed doomed to failure, for beyond their attire, and in particular the telling brassard they were obliged to wear on their sleeves, they seemed quite unremarkable.

Nicolae had quickly become bored with the view from the window and his attention was turning to our fellow passengers once more. I could fathom no harm in this and elected to conspire with him in his innocent ambition, seeking to draw Mama's attention with casual confabulation.

I remarked variously on the view, or the train's motion, but my efforts were to ill-effect, for her mood just then was not one to enter into talk for the sake of it. Eventually, I was obliged to pursue a more substantive conversation, partly to occupy her, partly through boredom.

"Mama, where is it again you said we were bound?"

"Bucharest, Anca. Surely you have not forgotten already?"

"No, I mean after Bucharest. The strange sounding name you mentioned."

"Really, Anca, why this sudden interest? Does it matter where? It could be in the very heart of the Transylvanian mountains for all I care, just so long as we can make a fresh start and begin to live normal lives again." She clutched my hands with gentle fingers. "I honestly cannot remember just now, Anca."

"I am curious, that is all. Is it not on the travel documents you were given?"

My persistence paid off, for with an impatient sigh Mama reluctantly rummaged through her purse and produced the relevant papers, passing them across. She smiled triumphantly at me, her point made. "You see, Anca, they are as meaningless to you as to me, unless you have suddenly acquired fluency in German."

"I can read German, a little."

It was a man's voice, from the end of the carriage. I looked up to see the bearded Jew hesitantly addressing us.

"Forgive my intrusion, but the carriage is small and I could not help but overhear. If... If you will permit me, perhaps I can translate the document for you."

I saw Mama freeze at his words, not daring to turn and confront him.

I whispered, "It is okay, Mama. Trust me. Please."

She declined to answer, but rather looked away, a sudden keen interest in the scenery. I got up and hesitantly made my way along the carriage to where the family of Jews sat, holding out the documents before me like a peace offering.

The man smiled as I reached him, taking the papers in one hand and gesturing with the other for me to sit down. I did so hesitantly, my eyes dancing from the man and his family to the door adjoining the next carriage, fearful that we might be interrupted.

"Do not worry, my friend. I understand your concern, but we will have ample notice should a guard venture this way, rest assured. Now, let me see what you have here."

His eyes scanned the documents briefly, then he put the papers down on his knee and smiled again. "My name if Chaim," he announced. "This is my wife, Golda, and our daughter, Elone." He glanced at the document again. "And you must be Anca, accompanying your mother and brother. Do not fear," he added, seeing my look of surprise. "Your names are listed on the document, that is all. And as to your question – your destination is the same as ours. We are all bound for Krakow."

"Poland?" Mama's reticence was forgotten at this announcement. She looked anxiously across the carriage. "You are mistaken, surely?"

Chapter 16.

Chaim referred to the document again, to reassure himself. "No, it is clearly stated. You are to be met at Krakow and taken from there to the resettlement camp, just as we are."

"As you are? But you are Jews." Mama could not hide her incredulous tone.

Chaim took no offence at my mother's observation. "My understanding is that it is a temporary measure, providing us with employment and a means of supporting our families, until the war is over. I am given to believe people are being brought to such camps from across Europe. Jew and Gentile alike. At any rate, we are to be travel companions for the duration of this journey. Will you then not sit with us?"

"Come, Mama, there is plenty of room here." I gestured to my mother to join us, but she declined the offer. Nicolae, however, had no such reservations, and ran across to take a seat next to the young girl and in an instant they were playing as if life-long friends. The man's wife, Golda, entreated Mama further, and reluctantly my mother joined us.

Thus befriended, the journey became a far more pleasant experience, despite the many hours that passed. Whenever we stopped for fuel or water, or pulled into a station, our families instantly separated, without notice or resort to explanation, fearful that a third party might enter the carriage, but we quickly re-joined as one as the journey continued and a bond of unlikely camaraderie was formed.

The family were better prepared than we, for they had brought refreshments with them, and these they shared with us without hesitation, although only little Nicolae, unburdened by the politics of manners, felt able to partake whole-heartedly given that we were unable to reciprocate their kind gesture.

As day turned to night and the train thundered through the still countryside our two families slowly became more open with one another until, at length, we were all, even Mama, relaxed in one another's company.

Chapter 17.

The Jewish family, it transpired, were themselves from Constanta, and they delighted in my retelling of my holiday there to convalesce after my malady some years previous. Even Mama became enthused as our discussions continued.

The execution of Papa received a genuinely sympathetic hearing for perhaps the first time, Golda clasping Mama to her, sharing her tears, and I could tell Mama felt better for this. In turn we heard of how the Jewish family, their relatives and friends had suffered persecution by first the Iron Guard, then the Nazis.

Until now I had thought the execution of my father to be the single most unpleasant event I might conceivably experience, but the stories Chaim related to us served to remind me that Papa's death was no isolated incident. That across the world what were once civilised countries were fast degenerating into barbarism.

"I pray to God that I am wrong," Chaim finished, taking my hand in his, his grip gentle and reassuring, his eyes apologetic to the heavens above. "But I fear we have offended Him, for He does not answer our prayers. Perhaps our resettlement will be a new beginning for us all. I dearly hope so."

He turned to me. "But Anca, my child, take nothing on trust. We are Jews, I know, and our way is not yours, but listen to my words carefully and heed them always."

His grip tightened, as if to add weight to what he was about to say.

"Whatever you see when we get to Bucharest, child, divert your eyes. Do not let your emotions dictate to you, no matter how much it hurts to look away. Do as you are told, when you are told, without question. Nothing more, nothing less. Promise me you will keep your little brother constantly at your side, and your hand clasped always to your mother's arm."

I looked into his eyes and saw tears forming. I had never seen a man cry before this day, yet first Maxim and now Chaim did so before me. Tears flooded my own eyes in empathy.

"Perhaps, my child... Just perhaps... We will see each other again when this war is over, and we can be friends openly, as the two children are already." He gestured to Nicolae and Elone, sleeping peacefully against one another.

Then he released his grip, glancing out of the window. "But for now, we are shortly to arrive in Bucharest. Hereon we must act once again as if we are total strangers. Goodbye, my friends. And God bless."

Before I could gather my thoughts to construct a reply the lights of Bucharest station were illuminating our carriage, parting salutations were being hurriedly exchanged and I felt Mama anxiously dragging sleepy Nicolae and myself away as the train ground to a shuddering halt. Nicolae objected loudly, his friendship with the girl abruptly and inexplicably terminated, but Mama's harsh words of admonishment ensured he stayed at our side, while Elone was likewise directed by her own parents, though not without noisy protest.

We sat quietly, awaiting instructions from the guard.

Chapter 18.

The station at Bucharest was a far more substantial affair than that of Medgidia, with an impressive architecture of balustrade, column and canopy that appeared somehow to keep the worst of the weather at bay whilst still efficiently dissipating the steam and smoke from the myriad locomotives that had converged beneath its vast ceiling. Even so the smell of creosote and engine oil combined to assail my olfactory senses in almost overpowering fashion.

Eventually, the guard arrived at our carriage, attending first the Jewish family. He directed them to disembark from the train and go to a building on the far side of the station, where other Jews were also bound. They followed his instructions without question, only young Elone turning to glance in our direction before her mother grabbed her arm and pulled the confused child to her side.

The guard turned to us, but I did not take in the exchange between him and my mother, my own attentions drawn in watching the Jews, for I could fathom no logic in separating them now if we were all bound for the same destination. I heard Mama's voice rise as she challenged the guard's directions.

"All night? Surely you are mistaken? I have two children with me."

"I am sorry."

"No. This is not acceptable. Why were we not told in advance?"

The guard lowered his voice. "Please, for your children's sake, do not cause a scene."

"But this cannot be right," Mama insisted. "Why, even the Jews are being taken to a place of comfort. Surely that cannot – "

"Be quiet, woman!" The guard cut her short with a sharp retort. "I do not make the rules. Would you rather argue your case with the Gestapo?"

Mama's indignation subsided at this thinly veiled threat. I clasped her arm and looked the guard in the eye. "Please, my mother is tired. She means no offence. Is that not right, Mama?" I shook my mother's hand, silently pleading with her not to pursue her grievance. A Gestapo officer was watching from a distance. Mama must have espied his attention, for she nodded her head, and clutched Nicolae to her side.

"You are wise, child," the guard said. "Try to sleep, now, that the night will pass by quickly. You will receive further instructions at dawn." The door slammed behind him, leaving us alone in the carriage.

Resigned to our fate we tried to make ourselves comfortable as best we could, now doubly grateful for the repast we had been allowed to share with the Jewish family during the course of our travel.

Fortunately, the journey had tired us all immensely and Nicolae, though at first inquisitive of the station's activity and then mindful of the absence of his new friend, quickly found comfort in slumber, his head resting upon my mother's lap.

I volunteered my coat as a blanket for him, resigned to spending the night quietly shivering in the cold carriage while assuring Mama I was quite comfortable, for fear she would insist I take her own.

Despite the discomfort of the narrow wooden benches I too finally succumbed to sleep and, for a welcome change, found pleasant memories to occupy my dreams.

Chapter 19.

It is the way of dreams that sometimes they become your waking reality. Thus it was for me on this occasion. For uncounted hours I had revelled in joys past, dancing in the spume of the Black Sea, young and carefree, with Mama and Nicolae and, of course, dear Papa.

But, as all good things must come to an end so, eventually it was time for us to go home. As I relived our return, boarding the train, relishing the excitement of the station, the flush of steam, the screech of locomotive wheels against the rails, dream mingled with reality and suddenly the slamming carriage doors in distant Constanta were slamming carriage doors in war-torn Bucharest.

It took a few seconds for me to shake the remnants of the past from my mind and as l did so I saw Mama's face before me, smiling as she spoke, although her words were not yet audible.

Suddenly I was being shaken by the shoulder and I sat up in an instant, banishing all but reality from my mind as I realized it was Nicolae, anxious to rouse me.

"Wake up Anca! Wake up! We have to get off now!"

We quickly joined the crowds gathering on the station concourse, fearful that we might miss vital instructions and be left stranded at Bucharest.

Uniformed officers barked orders in German, Romanian and other languages I could not identify. We were told to form a line to one side of the square, where it appeared we were being grouped either by nationality or language. Those slow to respond were angrily harassed by Nazi officers impatient of the very young, the elderly or the infirm, and I was shocked to witness people beaten with rifle butts if they were tardy.

Satisfying myself that Mama had Nicolae secure beneath her coat I remembered Chaim's advice and resolved to look down, clasping my mother's arm with one hand, dragging our trunk with the other.

Joining a group of my countrymen we stood and waited, anxiously watching the crowds divide. The Gestapo officers became increasingly irritated with those still unplaced, shouting violently in German as if raising their voices might transcend the barrier of language, but I could no more make sense of their orders than the confused civilians receiving them.

A gun shot rang out beneath the canopy. I heard a scream and the station at once fell silent, all attention upon a Gestapo officer in the centre of the square, standing over the prostrate body of a man, a still smoking pistol in his hand.

The body lay as it had fallen, a pool of blood forming around the head. As my eyes took in the scene my legs felt weak and nausea began to rise from my stomach. A sobbing woman broke away from the civilians restraining her and threw herself upon the dead man, shouting hysterically at the officer who had fired the shot. It was not a language I recognized, though I heard someone behind me mutter quietly that she was a Magyar, from Hungary.

I turned to Mama in confusion, surprised to find her facing away, comforting Nicolae beneath her coat, shielding him from the obscenity that was taking place nearby.

"Turn away, Anca," I heard Mama say. "Do not let them see you stare. Just stand quietly. It will be over soon."

With Mama and Nicolae safe beside me my thoughts turned to Chaim, his wife Golda and the sweet child Elone, whom Nicolae had so recently befriended. I scanned the concourse for any sign of them, aware for the first time there were no Jews anywhere to be seen.

Before I could gather my thought there was a commotion once more where the dead man lay and I watched in horror as two Iron Guard officers took the feet of the dead man and unceremoniously dragged away the body, leaving a trail of smeared blood in its wake.

The chaos and noise of the concourse had been replaced by sober order and sombre silence, broken only by the woman's hysterical sobs. For the rest of us, we merely stood and watched, not knowing what to expect. Not knowing what we could have done to help.

Fear hung over us, tangible as a dense smog.

Chapter 20.

As is if the incident had never happened, officers now began addressing each group in their own language, an Iron Guard lieutenant standing before our own small crowd of perhaps two hundred Romanians, dictating instructions for the next phase of our journey.

I focused my attention on his words, anxious that we should not contravene an instruction and reap the wrath of the Gestapo.

"The trains will shortly be arriving to escort you to Krakow, from where you will be transferred to your respective camps for resettlement," the lieutenant informed us. "Keep your documents safely with you, as these confirm your final destination. I regret the journey will not be pleasant, for space is limited and the distance long. We expect your quiet and orderly cooperation at this difficult time. Women and children will be separated from the men for the journey."

The lieutenant raised his hand to quell the murmur of objection.

"Quiet! You will be separated, women and children in one train, men in another. This is for your own convenience, to avoid the need to share the limited toilet facilities, nothing more. The sooner you arrive at the camp the sooner you will be reunited with your families. Warm showers, clean clothing and hot soup will await you on arrival."

A murmur of relief ran through the crowd at this news. Someone demanded, "Just how long will the journey take?"

The Iron Guard officer shrugged nonchalantly. "No questions, please. In a moment you will be provided with chalk. Please mark your luggage clearly with your names. Your luggage, too, will be carried separately, to make your journey more comfortable. Once labelled it will be collected here, and returned to you on arrival at your destination."

Station workers appeared before us and handed out misshapen stumps of chalk. I took a piece and inscribed our family name, Pasculata, with meticulous care on the side of our trunk. As I did so Mama knelt beside me saying, "Anca, please, my diary. I must have it by my side."

I knew how important Mama's diary was to her and quickly raised the lid, retrieving the precious journal for her with seconds to spare before a station worker gripped the jute handle and began to drag the case away.

"One moment!" I shouted, and locked the trunk lid securely, fearful that our few possessions might be lost during transit. Bad enough that our luggage should leave our side at all, for it was all we had. As if echoing my own fears I heard an angry voice behind me remonstrate with the Iron Guard officer.

"What if it is lost?" a man of ruddy complexion angrily demanded, one foot planted firmly on his valise. "It contains all my family's belongings. Personal items of sentimental value. I prefer to carry my trunk with me."

The Iron Guard lieutenant turned on the man, hurling abuse in a raised voice, warning him to remove his foot and do as he were told. His words were impolite and I shall not repeat here other than a summary of the exchange, for the man behind me was not lightly deterred, and angrily challenged the officer's authority.

As he did so I felt Mama's hand on my arm, drawing me to the back of the crowd, putting distance between us and the two antagonists. I followed meekly, mesmerized by the argument raging just a few metres away.

"You are a traitor," I heard the man declare, his voice laden with venom. "You wear the uniform of our country yet perform the deeds of these... These animals."

"Do not try my patience, old man," the officer warned, looking anxiously about him. "I follow orders, nothing more."

"Orders? They are the orders of the devil incarnate!"

The lieutenant looked bewildered. "Be quiet, you fool, and do as I say." He glanced round to see the eyes of the Gestapo on him. He lowered his voice. "Do you not understand, old man? I have no choice in this, any more than you do."

The defiant older man raised his voice still louder. "I understand entirely. You are a traitor! You throw in your hand with these evil swine to protect your own cowardly hide!"

"Quiet!" screamed the lieutenant, angrily drawing a pistol from his holster. "Silence or I will shoot."

As the officer brandished the weapon the station fell silent once more. Mama pulled me back, Nicolae thrust even further beneath her coat. She urged me in loud whispers to look away, but I could not.

The sentiments being voiced, even the words used, were strangely familiar and I realized these phrases, of treachery and cowardice, were just those I had heard Papa use in his argument with the Iron Guard in Medgidia, outside our home. A week later Papa was dead, executed by firing squad, his crime to challenge the authority of the Iron Guard and their Nazi leaders. I wanted to go to this man, to calm him, to warn him, to let him know of Papa's fate, but fear rooted me to the spot.

The man stood defiant against the officer even as those around him moved away, distancing themselves for their own safety, the attention of the entire station by now directed on this exchange. The man's wife begged him to back down. Their daughter, only a little younger than I, was crying hysterically, and the woman tried to comfort her while at the same time pleading with her husband.

"Gheorghe, please, no! For God's sake, no! Do as they say. The trunk is unimportant. It is of no consequence."

If the man called Gheorghe heard his wife he paid no heed, but stood firm against the Iron Guard lieutenant. Two men placed themselves around the woman and daughter and slowly edged them away. The woman struggled against them, the girl screaming.

Now the man called Gheorghe and the Iron Guard officer stood face to face, one arrogant, armed with a pistol, the other defenceless yet bravely, foolishly defiant. A Gestapo officer strode across and confronted the two. The lieutenant turned, raising his arm and stamped his feet in the Nazi salute.

The defiant Gheorghe spat angrily into the dust at his feet. "Traitor! I am ashamed to call you my fellow countryman."

The Gestapo officer ignored him. "You have a problem, Herr Lieutenant?" he asked in broken Romanian.

"This man will not allow his trunk to be placed with the others," the Iron Guard officer reported, still hesitantly pointing his gun at the man before him.

The Nazi looked at the defiant Gheorghe contemptuously. He turned back to the Iron Guard officer and shrugged indifferently.

"Then shoot him."

At this order a gasp ran through our group and the man's wife screamed out, pleading to her husband to apologise and do as bid. Mama was tugging at me, urging me to look away, but I could not. It were as if my eyes were drawn, like magnets, towards the unfolding drama.

"He will not shoot," Gheorghe stated with quiet confidence. "We are both Romanians. He will not shoot one of his own countrymen, traitor though he may be."

The lieutenant's face paled, sweat breaking out across his forehead, the hand holding the pistol shook visibly.

The Gestapo officer smiled. "This is your chance to prove him wrong, Herr Lieutenant. Shoot him. Now. On my authority." He raised his voice. "Do it."

The Iron Guard officer stood motionless, his face demonstrating the transition of emotion from arrogance to fear. Suddenly the Gestapo officer drew his own pistol and pressed it to the head of the Iron Guard officer.

"Kill him, Herr Lieutenant, or I kill you."

Chapter 21.

For a few seconds it seemed even the locomotives had stopped, so quiet had the station become. Wife and daughter looked on in horror, unable even to scream. No-one dared breathe. Then, even as I watched, the Iron Guard lieutenant slowly tightened his finger on the trigger.

It was too much and I somehow managed to avert my eyes. A shot echoed around the station and blood splattered across the ground, almost to my feet. When I looked up the defiant Gheorghe was slumped face down on the ground, blood-imbrued clothes confirming the deed.

The lieutenant was still in position, the pistol in his outstretched hand, staring down and the man whose life he had just taken, his face ashen.

From the crowd, even from the man's wife and daughter, there was only stunned silence. No-one dared move. Slowly I raised my eyes to the Nazi officer, whose own pistol was still pressed to the head of the Iron Guard lieutenant.

"You see, it was easy," the Nazi told him. "As easy as this."

Without warning he pulled the trigger and the Iron Guard lieutenant fell where he stood, his body slumping next to the man whose life he had just taken. The second shot jolted us back to reality. No-one moved forward to intervene, but I knew I was not alone in falling to my knees, my legs unable to take my weight, fighting back the convulsions in my stomach. Forcing myself to look up I saw the Gestapo officer turn to us, his face, his voice, devoid of emotion.

"Now, you will place your trunks as directed. Then you will await further instructions. In total silence. Is that clear? One more foolish outburst and I will kill that child."

At random he pointed his gun to a young girl nearby. The child screamed and her mother threw herself around her daughter, sobbing quietly, not daring to release her emotions more fully. Then the Nazi spun on his heels and walked away, barking orders in German, returning the station to a state of furious activity.

I wanted to go to the bereaved woman and her daughter, to offer comfort, but fear prevented my limbs from moving. I just knelt as I had fallen and watched, not even able to cry, as the two bodies were dragged away. No-one dared speak. No-one dared look the other in the eye. It were as if every emotion at once were fighting for release, but fear and shock dominated, suppressing all others and I found myself staring blankly at the blood soaking into the dust of the station floor. Mama refused to turn round, hugging Nicolae beneath her coat, trying desperately to comfort him and dissuade his interest.

I longed for something to disturb the quiet which had now befallen the station and in this at least, found reward, for amidst shouted orders in German I saw the doors of the far building open and from there emerged, in single file, the Jews. I scanned the queue desperately for sign of the family that had so recently befriended us and at length saw Golda and little Elone, looking tired and fearful, emerge from the building. At this point I realized there were only women and children present. Of Chaim, of all the Jewish men, there was no sign.

Behind us the noise of locomotive activity drew our attention and I saw an enormous engine drawing what appeared to be cattle trucks into the station, in a procession at least twenty wagons long and behind which another engine of similar size pulled a similar cargo. At first I was mystified, for some of the truck doors were open, demonstrating they were empty, yet there was no evidence of cattle at the station awaiting transportation.

The mystery was quickly to be resolved however, for barely had the train stopped than the lines of Jews received new instructions and began filing across, boarding these same wagons.

Those that had difficulty mounting the vehicle were forcefully pushed or thrown on by Gestapo officers and when the truck appeared quite full to capacity still more Jews were pushed on, until the doors had literally to be forced shut, every last inch of space occupied.

As one truck filled the next was opened. When young children or the infirm or elderly stumbled or met difficulty mounting the wagon, Gestapo officers pistol-whipped them or set about them with their rifle butts, knocking them to the ground, then forcing them to get up and continue the embarkation.

I watched with mounting horror as this scene unfolded, struck equally by the brutality of the Nazis and by the fearful unwillingness of any civilian to intervene.

As I focused upon Golda's and Elone's plight I felt ashamed at my own inaction, but even though my mind considered possible means of assistance, my body simply refused to respond, ridden by fear, so soon after seeing three men killed before my eyes. If their bodies had been dragged away, their blood still stained the ground, a congealing memorial to their untimely demise.

By now Golda and Elone were at the side of a wagon, waiting to climb aboard. I watched, mortified, as Golda lifted her little daughter onto the train and threw my hands to my face in horror as the little girl lost her grip on the cold steel and fell to the floor, screaming in pain. As Golda bent to pick her up a Gestapo officer swung at the mother with his rifle, knocking her to the ground. I started forward instinctively, but an unknown hand on my shoulder restrained me and I took control of my anger.

Now, unbelievably, the Nazi began to set about poor Elone as she lay crying on the floor, screaming abuse at her in German, each sentence accompanied by a vicious kick from his jackboots. So horrified was I by this scene that my eyes seemed to view the events in slow motion, each kick witnessed in obscene detail, my eyes following the action but my other senses dulled, my body somehow unable to respond.

Elone's mother screamed at the Nazi as she tried to rescue the child from this brutal assault, but he simply kicked her away and then began again to viciously set about the child, shouting incoherently in German as he did so, each sentence matched by another callous attack with the heel of his jackboot.

"Nicolae!"

The name screeched from behind me, the shout breaking the spell and I turned to see my mother screaming hysterically, being restrained with difficulty by several men, fearful for her safety.

Utterly confused I turned again to the scene across the square and felt my heart all but stop as the subject of Mama's hysteria became apparent. For there, racing across the concourse towards Elone, my little brother Nicolae was in full pelt, about to launch the might of his six year old frame against the Nazi officer assaulting his friend.

Chapter 22.

For what seemed like an eternity I stood cataleptic, unable to believe my eyes, as my brother ran across the square and threw himself, screaming, at the offending officer, clinging to his uniform and battering him with his tiny fists.

It were as if I were in a trance, for I could do nothing but watch, though my only thoughts were to protect Nicolae from harm. Around me the stunned attention of the entire station was focused on this small child.

As I struggled to grasp what was happening my fears were for Nicolae's very life, as the Nazi reached down and grabbed my brother's arms. The next thing I was conscious of I had broken free of the restraining hands on my shoulder and was myself in full flight across the station, running faster than I could ever imagine, screaming my Nicolae's name.

The officer held the defiant child in the air at arms length, Nicolae's tiny arms and legs flailing wildly in a futile attempt to release himself. I stopped a few metres from them, not knowing what to do.

Not knowing what I could do.

Around us there was silence everywhere, everyone watching, waiting. Even Nicolae's screams had subsided, his exhausted larynx unable to raise a syllable more, the dawning reality of his predicament introducing terror where anger had previously ruled.

Suddenly Mama found her own voice and shouted across the station from where she was being restrained, screaming for the officer to put her son down. Even as I turned in her direction I saw an Iron Guard officer raise his rifle and bring the butt down forcefully upon her head. I watched horrified as blood erupted across her temple and Mama collapsed to the floor. I was too far distant to know the extent of her injury and dared not react for fear the same treatment would be meted out upon Nicolae.

Still there was silence. No-one dared move.

Then without warning the Gestapo officer holding Nicolae began to laugh. It was a cold, cruel laugh, as if he found his assault by a six year old boy genuinely amusing. Other Gestapo officers joined in and the atmosphere lightened tangibly as their laughter resounded around the previously silent station, Iron Guard officers hesitantly following suit.

The civilian crowd looked on in anxious silence, fearful for their and our, safety.

Mine and Nicolae's eyes were as one, united in fear and apprehension, not daring to move, not knowing what response to anticipate.

Speaking in loud, barked German, the Nazi addressed his fellow officers to yet more laughter, the joke apparently at our expense, then suddenly he turned and effortlessly flung my brother's tiny frame into the cattle wagon.

Screaming Nicolae's name, I was in an instant climbing aboard to affect his rescue, forcing my way past Elone and Golda, my only thought to reach Nicolae.

I found him laying dazed on the floor of the truck and tended him as best I could, but found myself being pushed to the rear of the wagon as more Jews were forced aboard.

Desperately I stood up, holding Nicolae for fear he would be crushed. I struggled to see beyond them to where Mama had fallen and my heart leapt as I glimpsed her being helped to her feet. The sight of blood running down my mother's face from a head wound was the last thing I saw as the doors slammed shut, plunging us into darkness.

~

The adult bodies on all sides threatened to crush me, for my twelve years told against me in height and strength. I clutched Nicolae as tightly as I could, unable to move my arms to comfort him, unable to see his face in the darkness to ascertain his well-being. I tried desperately to solicit help of those around me, but none spoke Romanian, or if they did they chose to ignore my pleas. I called out to Golda and Elone, but no reply came, if indeed they were in the same wagon.

Eventually I heard the sound of engines warming and knew we would soon commence our journey. I prayed it would be short.

Suddenly the wagon lurched as the locomotive heaved into motion, sending a wave of instability through the train. Around me I felt people struggle for balance and heard screams as some fell.

A hand clutched my leg, but I dared not let go of Nicolae to reach down and seconds later the grip slowly released. What became of those who fell I could only imagine. I shut their cries from my mind and concentrated all my thoughts on holding my brother steady. Nothing else, no-one else, mattered.

Eventually the train steadied, gathering speed as we departed Bucharest. Despite the darkness, the overpowering body-heat and the stale air, relaxation was not an option for me, for I knew if I allowed Nicolae or myself to fall we would not rise again.

As countless hours passed, thirst and a heavy bladder increasingly dominated my needs, for there was no possibility of refreshment or relief in these dire circumstances. As fatigue took its toll, it became more and more difficult to keep my eyes open. I desperately wanted to sleep, for in doing so I hoped to find temporary release from the discomfort, but dared not risk us falling.

Each time I allowed my eyes to close images of the brutal attacks upon Elone and Mama quickly filled my mind and I found myself sobbing uncontrollably. In my present state of nervous shock I was, I concluded, particularly prone to bad dreams.

But in truth, as I was soon to realise, the nightmare was only just beginning.

Chapter 23.

Poland, I was vaguely aware, lay far to the north of the Transylvanian Alps, perhaps even beyond the distant Carpathians. Such a tramontane journey at this time of year would have been arduous in the best of circumstances, let alone the dire condition we now found ourselves in.

I could only guess how much time passed as the early stoicism of my unseen fellow travellers gave way to pitiful moans of suffering as lack of air and water took its toll. Eventually, the noise seemed to subside as exhaustion overcame those around us.

Too dark to make out any form and unable to move other than my arms, which held Nicolae high, supported by the unwilling bodies on all sides, I could only imagine the cruel reality of the scene unfolding.

Through the inadequate air vents in the roof of the wagon, towards which all who could do so stretched their bodies to gain some small advantage, the light of day or night could just be determined and I counted four days and nights passed during which we remained crammed together in this dire condition. Stale air and sweat mingled inevitably with the stench of urine and excreta as the journey continued. Unable to move in any way there was of course no possibility of relief other than where we stood, and if at first thankful for the darkness, discomfort soon overcame any feeling of embarrassment or shame, for everyone there, adult and child alike, were similarly obliged.

My throat was parched, my tongue tumescent, and I knew Nicolae must be suffering similarly, although I could not see him, and dared not move my hands to comfort him for fear he slip between the crammed bodies to a certain death. He had made no sound all this while and I supposed he must be in shock. His torso still convulsed, but less violently than before, and his breathing had eased. Desperate as I was to hear him speak, at the same time I hoped he would not awaken from his trance too soon, to find himself in this fearful plight.

Around me the incessant low whine of suffering would be broken by louder outbursts as women and children cried out, though in pain or defiance I could not tell, for they spoke languages I could not identify and I soon came to ignore them as best I could. Not once did I hear a word uttered in my native Romanian.

Infrequently the train stopped, for fuel and water, perhaps even at stations to take on still more people. It was impossible to tell, for little was audible beyond the dull moans of those around me. Each stop was a moment of mixed emotions, first praying this would be the journey's end that we would be liberated from the obscene incarceration, then fear and despair as we began to move again. For a horrific pattern was emerging which was perhaps ultimately responsible for the survival of Nicolae and myself, though the cost to others was dear.

As the locomotive took the strain of its procession after each stop, with cold indifference to the suffering it drew in its wake, the train would lurch forward each time, throwing off balance the mass of bodies inside the wagons. In the dark I slowly came to realise that each time some among us fell or collapsed to the floor. Such were the screams of agony that haunted the darkness at these times, and our memories constantly since, I knew those who fell met a certain, slow death being crushed or suffocated.

Fear now kept me from even considering sleep and I waited anxiously for each stop, steadying myself with Nicolae in my arms in anticipation of the next jolt of the wagon as the journey recommenced. It was this realisation and preparation, I am sure, that served to keep us both alive.

Many were the occasions an unseen body fell near my feet and desperate hands clutched at my legs, trying to raise themselves from the tangle of bodies below. My reaction was, at best, one of calculated inaction, once even shaking off clutching fingers so small they could only have been a child's, for the survival of Nicolae and myself was by now my only thought, heedless of the fate of those around me. In this I was perhaps aided by my indifference to their tongue, for had I understood their pleading as they slipped away, I doubt I could have maintained my cruel isolation so easily.

Even so, I knew I could not continue much longer, for Nicolae grew heavier as I grew weaker and, as the bodies around me fell or were dragged down so I was less able to use others as support.

Often I wondered if it would not be better to concede defeat and allow ourselves to sink down into the mire of death at our feet, to end our suffering.

Had I been alone I might have taken this option, for I feared such an end would shortly become us regardless, but I knew I could not make that decision for Nicolae. His survival was paramount, for I had promised Papa I would look after him, and at this time my little brother was completely dependent on my own tenacious grasp of life.

Chapter 24.

The days passed and still my little brother did not awaken from his torpor. At one stage I managed to free my hand enough to trace the contours of his face. His eyes were closed, I could tell, and for this I was grateful, but as my fingers touched his dry, chapped lips and swollen tongue I knew I must do something to ease his suffering. I tried to cry, that my tears might moisten his lips, but my body was too exhausted to respond to my emotions.

In desperation my free hand squeezed his wet underclothes, my fingers smearing the fetid urine across his lips, moistening the broken skin. I tried to whisper comforting words to him, but could not manage even this simple task, my own mouth so deformed by dehydration. I reached down again and brought the foul moisture to my own lips, savouring the relief it gave.

Eventually the train fell almost silent, as those around me succumbed to the inevitable. Those standing grew fewer and fewer by the hour, and we found ourselves struggling to keep balance among what I knew must be the corpses of our fellow passengers at our feet.

Then, soon after I had watched the night's sable darkness turn to blue dawn through the tiny vent above us, on the fifth day, it happened.

The sound came first, in the distance, a loud explosion that shattered the silence. From what direction I could not divine, my mind too numb even to register the event clearly. Then the motion of the train seemed to alter slightly. There was a rumbling, then loud crashing sounds and the piercing squeal of metal against metal. Our wagon began lurching from side to side, throwing us off balance and in a second I had lost Nicolae, his body parted from mine.

Panic overtook me and I managed to scream out his name, diving down, clutching at bodies, desperate to find him, in the darkness unable to identify the bodies beneath me. I grabbed wildly at limbs on all sides, hoping somehow to recognize my brother's tiny form, acutely aware that many I touched were cold and lifeless.

Nicolae I knew, had been warm, at least. Alive, if only just.

I found a child's body and my heart leapt, but it was cold and I pushed it to one side indifferently as the wagon rocked violently about me.

Suddenly the floor seemed to rise beneath my feet and I was flying through the air, coming crashing to a painful halt against the roof of the upturned wagon.

The carriage was flooded with light as the side of the wagon ripped open and for a split-second my eyes, all but blinded by the light of day, registered the scene of carnage around me, a tangle of wounded bodies and filth-ridden corpses, women and children alike, some still alive, just, but many clearly, thankfully, beyond feeling.

And then pain overwhelmed me, darkness enveloped me, and I slipped into unconsciousness.

The respite was short-lived. I could not have lain there more than a few minutes when the sound of gunfire penetrated my mind, returning me instantly to cruel reality.

My eyes opened to the same scene of devastation I had just witnessed, but this time I was not to be blessed with the protective curtain of comatose oblivion.

The horror of the obscenity before me sank home slowly, my eyes unable to liberate themselves from the magnetic draw of the carnage on all sides. There were few signs of life, and none of the survivors were able to free themselves. I scanned the bodies for some sign of Nicolae, but if he were there among them I did not recognise him.

In the distance I could hear the staccato sound of machine-gun fire drawing closer, but had no way of knowing its origin or target. I tried to move but bodies were strewn over me in an obscene tangle of bloodied limbs, pinning me down

As I struggled to free myself, the face of a young child, barely Nicolae's age, fell down to hang in front of me, lifeless eyes staring from a bloodied skull, the torso wedged above me between heavy timbers that had once formed the frame of the wagon. I tried to scream but no sound came. I tried to back away but my body had not the strength to retreat from this obscenity that hung pendent before me.

For untold minutes I lay in shock, staring back at these dulled eyes before my own, thankful only that the body was not that of Nicolae or Elone, yet acutely aware they might share a similar fate somewhere beside me.

The barbarous rattle of machine-gun fire drew closer and I heard the sound of shouts in German between the bouts of firing. Screams were cut short by the staccato bursts but I could only guess at what was happening, as I fought desperately to liberate my body from its prison of tangled corpses.

Then suddenly my speculation was redundant for a Nazi soldier came into view and without warning began to spray our wagon with machine-gun fire. My body arched instinctively, but I could do nothing but watch in abject horror as the spray of bullets drew closer, sweeping the pile of bodies before me, extinguishing the life of the survivors.

Even as realisation dawned I was about to die, the machine-gun fire was upon me. A spray of bullets ripped into the lifeless corpse that hung before me in an explosion of flesh and blood.

Pain seared through me as the bullets found my own body, and my last thought, as blood cascaded over me from the cadaver above, was one of relief that it was, at last, over. Nicolae must surely have perished already and in this certain knowledge death was no longer feared but welcomed.

Eager now to join my brother, I lapsed, gently, into the dark night.

Chapter 25.

Of nominally Orthodox upbringing, I had no real idea of what the after-life might bring, certain only that it must be better than the existence I had just departed.

As if to confirm this supposition I felt a pleasing sensation on my lips, for a minute unfamiliar, then recognized to be cool, clean water. I felt the fluid seep between the teeth and onto my tumescent tongue and knew that I must be in heaven, for only there, surely, could one conceivably experience such sybaritic pleasure.

I savoured the moment. Words cannot describe how beautiful the taste of such commonplace a commodity as water after so many days of enforced abstinence.

Then I remembered Nicolae and all thought of heaven vanished, reality imposing its presence in an instant. I felt more of the precious liquid being applied to my chapped lips and instinctively pushed myself away, for my bodily needs were as nothing compared to my concern for my sibling.

I felt a gentle hand at my head restrain me and a voice spoke, the tone soft and reassuring, the language unfamiliar. I lay still while my mind sifted myriad unfocused images that fought for my attention. I tried to call out Nicolae's name but pain seared through my body at the attempt and I fell back, exhausted even by this feeble effort.

Again I tried to speak, but a finger gentle against my lips prohibited my ambition, the stranger's words surely urging me to be still and silent.

I felt water again applied to my lips and this time I tried to move my swollen tongue to savour it, hoping to draw strength from its refreshing powers.

If my vision was slowly beginning to focus, still nothing seemed clear. I could see daylight around me and from above could ascertain the amorphous image of a tree swaying gently in the breeze. But of my benefactor, indeed of anyone, I could see nothing.

I inhaled deeply, partaking of the cool, clean air, savouring the contrast as I remembered the feculence of the past days.

Gently cupped hands tilted before my face and I felt more of the cool fluid run over my lips and cheeks, and down my neck. As the water trickled slowly down my parched and arid throat, I felt my whole body strengthen in response.

A hand at my head lowered me until I was resting on what I smelt to be grass, though I could not move my neck enough to see it. Above me I saw a blurred figure move away. I tried to call out but the task was beyond me and I reluctantly accepted my fate, laying still, for every attempt to move wracked my body with pain. Desperate as I was to know the fate of my brother all I could do was pray that Nicolae too had been rescued with me. My eyelids were heavy and, overcome with fatigue, I lapsed once more.

When next I opened my eyes it was dusk, but pain still wracked my body and I fell back into slumber seconds later, vaguely conscious as I did so of a fire burning a short way distant. The flames seem to carry into my sleep for fire dominated my dreams over the next few hours until, at length, I awoke again, this time finding the pain more tolerable, and slowly I opened my eyes to the night.

The only illumination was now provided by the fire, its heavenly flames dancing gently to the unheard rhythm of the evening's breeze, but still my muscles would not respond enough to permit me to turn.

Perhaps attracted by my efforts, an unfocused figure again appeared above me, leaning over my prostrate form. The blur came closer until it was just above me, hovering like an angel, though I had by now dismissed such flights of fancy from my mind.

The face came slowly into focus, first the eyes, then the other features, the contours flickering gently in the fire's lambent illumination. Small fingers reached out and touched my face, and as they did so I felt my eyes moisten. Defying the pain a smile spread across cracked lips and my hand raised to take the fingers that lay on my cheek.

I felt Nicolae's hand in mine and the tears became torrents as pent emotions were released in unquestioning gratitude.

I raised my other arm, clutching my little brother tight, drawing his body against mine. Tears of pain mingled with the tears of joy that flooded my cheeks, but I held him closer still, determined never to let him go. I wanted desperately to caress the sores on his lips, to offer comfort and tender his hollow cheeks, but I could not bring myself to let go the tight grip I held him in, for fear he might disappear, that his very presence might prove to be an illusion.

"Anca, why are you crying?"

Nicolae's words were mellifluent, his question innocence incarnate, and for some minutes I could do nothing but attempt to smile through my tears. I tried to plant a kiss upon his cheek, but painful lips made me recoil. As my tears began to subside I tried again to speak, but words were not yet possible and I lay back again, now secure in the knowledge my little brother, at least, was safe.

Of Mama... Of Chaim and Golda, and of the sweet child Elone... Of the countless innocents that had been on the train with us... Of these I could not know, taking small comfort from the thought that we surely could not be the sole survivors.

An unknown figure approached and gently eased Nicolae to his feet, evidently suggesting I should be left to recuperate. Knowing Nicolae to be in safe hands I acquiesced without further objection, determined to rest now, that I might find the strength to rise when next I woke.

Chapter 26.

Distant voices drifted across my mind, chasing an already forgotten dream from my consciousness. There were male and female voices both, and I fancied I could tell of varying ages. Some were in languages I did not recognize but too were some, at least, in my native Romanian.

I happily recognized Nicolae's voice among them, calling out to someone, and for a minute or two I lay listening to them, trying to make sense of their fleeting conversations.

I could feel the sun's warmth on my face, daylight once again upon us. My eyes flickered open, adjusting slowly to the brightness. Above me the tree stood proud, its branches swaying gently in a light breeze scented by a confetti of cascading pastel blossoms that evoked cheering memories of halcyon days. An effulgent sun stood proud in the sky above.

My anxieties of the previous night were gone, for I knew Nicolae to be safe, and as yet concern about Mama was not heavy upon my mind. I felt relaxed in my decumbent position, though I remembered well the pain that attempts at movement had wrought upon me previously. Nonetheless I resolved to defy such discomfort this morning and rise shortly to investigate my circumstances.

I lay still a little longer, enjoying the sun's warmth and allowing my strength to build, then with slow, cautious movements, made as if to sit up. Searing pain ran through my shoulder at the attempt and I cried out, throwing my body onto one side to try and escape the torment that beset me. All at once I heard a demulcent voice at my side and firm hands took me around the waist, raising me to a sitting position before tilting my body back to rest against the trunk of a tree.

The face of my benefactor now became apparent as he crouched before me, offering a welcome smile and comforting words, but his language was alien, only his tone making sense. He was dressed in peasant clothes yet around his waist an ammunition belt hung, and slung over his shoulder a rifle further challenged this bucolic first impression.

I tried to speak, for the tumescence had subsided and my tongue could at least move, but my lips were still sore, the skin broken and scab-ridden, my vocal chords not yet willing to respond to my will. Realising my bewilderment the man to my fore gestured to someone behind me, and seconds later another figure appeared, similarly attired to the first.

"Anca, how are you feeling now, child?" He spoke in hesitant, broken Romanian, but I was grateful for the familiar words.

I attempted an answer without success and raised my strong hand to my throat to indicate my plight. The man gestured his understanding and, turning to his friend, spoke quickly in a foreign tongue, after which the first man took his leave. The second turned to me again and ventured to explain himself.

"My name is Karol," he said slowly. "I speak only a little Romanian. I am sorry." He paused, as if uncertain I had understood him. I nodded for him to continue.

"Do you perhaps speak Polish, or German?"

I shook my head, braving the obtuse pain.

The man calling himself Karol shrugged in resignation. "Then I will try to my best to explain. First, your brother is safe and well, as you will by now know."

At Nicolae's mention I tried to look around that I might see him, but there was no sign within the limited range of my vision and pain prevented me searching further afield.

"He is in good hands," Karol assured me. "He is unhurt. You, however, must rest for many days. You have a... What is the word... An injury, to your shoulder. A bullet passed through you, but no vital organs were touched and you will soon heal. It was a lucky escape for you, Anca. There were very few survivors."

I nodded slowly. This news was not unexpected, but the confirmation was no easier for that.

He asked, "You are not Jewish?"

I shook my head.

"I thought not. Yet you were in the same wagon?"

Again I tried to speak, to explain, but quickly retired from the challenge. Witnessing my struggle Karol urged me to be silent.

"I will speak. You will listen."

I nodded again and Karol began a slow and laboured explanation of the events that had brought us together. "You will know already how you came to be on a train full of Jews. More so than I. How so is no longer important. Also you will perhaps know you were bound for Krakow, there to go on to a resettlement camp."

Again I nodded assent.

Karol paused, choosing his words carefully. "We struck at the train two days ago now. Some few kilometres west of here. Explosives beneath the tracks."

He saw my look of confusion at this news and added, "Please understand, child, you were not the target. It should not have been your train that we took out, though your fate can only be the better for it."

I looked into his eyes, trying to understand his meaning, but could make no sense of his reasoning. He was speaking again and I listened carefully.

"Unfortunately we returned too late to save many. The Nazis had already turned their weapons upon the survivors and left you for dead."

This much I knew already, for the image of the Nazi soldier firing upon us was not one I would soon forget.

"We tracked a few of them," Karol continued, "but most got away, over the border into Czechoslovakia."

He saw my surprise at this observation and ventured to add, "You are in Poland now, Anca, far from your own country. Perhaps when you are fully recovered you will wish to try and return to Romania? I cannot say what will be best for you."

I briefly considered the suggestion while my benefactor chose his next words.

If we had crossed the border then logic dictated Krakow could not be far, for I knew it to be a city in Poland. Whatsoever its distance, I knew that Mama was bound there, and that it must be our destination. But unable to communicate such sentiments I lay still, preserving my strength, concentrating once more as Karol continued his explanation.

"Anca, please try to understand. We can care for you for a few days, but no more. There are too many of you – about thirty in all – and we are not equipped for such a venture. Our comrades in the Resistance will be waiting for us. Already we are behind in our tasks."

The Resistance. I had heard this word whispered many times by Papa, before his execution. If I still did not understand who or what they were, I drew solace from the knowledge that Papa had spoken highly of them, although I knew such only from overheard snatches of conversations.

Karol spoke again. I was thankful for the pauses as he struggled to select his words, for it gave me time to organize my own thoughts.

He said, "But for now, child, you must rest. Your brother Nicolae is quite safe. He will come to you later. But only by resting will you have the strength to... To survive, once we are gone. So please, rest now. Build up your strength. My comrades will provide you with food and water, but they do not speak your language. We are all Poles or Slovaks, I am sorry. Please be patient."

He took my hand briefly, and then was gone, back into the undergrowth not far distant, and I was alone, looking forward to seeing Nicolae once more.

Chapter 27.

Over the next few days I affected a rapid recovery, my injuries treated with a sickly-smelling poultice that seemed to promote rapid healing.

My recovery was further encouraged by the realisation that little Elone had been among those few who had survived the massacre of the injured following the train derailment. I had to presume that Golda had perished either then or during the journey itself, for she was not numbered among the survivors there with us.

Of Chaim's fate, as my mother's, I had no knowledge. I did not even know if they had been on that train, though I knew their destination to be the same. Of course the likely fate of Elone's parents had not yet been imparted to the child, with whom I now found myself entrusted the care of, along with my little brother.

Had I realised then the full implications of this adoption I would perhaps have distanced myself from the prospect, but Nicolae and Elone had renewed their acquaintance during my period of convalescence and now were all but inseparable. Further, their friendship prevented either of them from dwelling too long on the fate of their respective parents, my half-hearted assurances that they would be soon re-united seemingly serving to satisfy them.

Thus it was inevitable that, when our benefactors declared it was time for them to leave us, I found myself burdened with both Nicolae and Elone as my sole responsibility. Not least this was because, among the survivors, only we three were Romanian by nationality. The others were Bulgars, Magyars and other Slav nationals, and all Jews, for what that mattered. These few, of the untold number on the train, survived. All the others had perished on the journey or been slaughtered by the Nazis after the crash.

My few days recuperating were, in the circumstances, enjoyably spent, our benefactors proving themselves fine hosts, despite the difficult communications.

My injuries were minor compared with some, although others, Nicolae and Elone included, seemed to have enjoyed a miraculous escape, having been buried beneath the bodies of others after the derailment and thus protected from the spray of bullets unleashed by the Nazi murderers. But even so, I knew many hundreds, perhaps thousands, had met their death during transit or by bullet at the journey's abrupt termination and this fact weighed heavy on my mind.

I learned that, once sure there were no further survivors among the wreckage, the Resistance had elected to give those who perished a mass cremation, destroying bodies and train as one in a fiery inferno, using fuel from a Nazi convoy previously hijacked.

This much Karol imparted to me during our infrequent conversations, and once my voice returned I managed to establish the vaguest of directions for Krakow.

I began making plans for Nicolae and I, with Elone in tow as I now realised we must, to pursue my mother's fate. Karol tried to convince me that return to my native Romania was in our best interests, but I would brook no such advice, and at length he abandoned his protests and supplied me with what little information he could.

I did not relish the prospect, with the burden of two young children, for Krakow was stated to be many hundreds of kilometres distant, even further into Poland than we currently found ourselves, and I knew my injured shoulder would oblige both children to make their own way, for carriage would not be possible.

Of course we had no money for food or shelter, bore only the clothes we stood in, cleaned but still ragged from the excesses of our journey, and had not even a command of the language to help us by.

But Karol aside no-one objected, for truth be told they were glad not to be burdened with three children themselves.

Thus it was, that soon after our benefactors had bid us good luck and disappeared into the forests to pursue their fight against the Nazis, I gather Nicolae and Elone around me and we hesitantly began the long trek north in pursuit of those we loved.

Chapter 28.

Our first days alone in the wilderness were to prove surprisingly easy, for the spring climate remained favourable, a warm wind rising from the south-west. We were blessed with clear skies of a day, the spring sun quickly warming the atmosphere, and clouded evenings that kept the night's temperature from dropping too low.

After the extreme discomfort we had so recently endured we found little problem sleeping, snuggling together beneath bushes for additional warmth, and countless sub-alpine streams provided cool, fresh water whenever we required it. Even when back in Medgidia we had grown used to eating unripe fruit and strange plants and, if we missed the luxury of a warm meal, this was no great hardship.

We followed a route approximating north-west, using the sun as our guide, always keeping the mountains behind us. Eventually I hoped to come across a road or railway that we could follow at a discreet distance in the hope of obtaining a keener direction.

By the second day I could stand it no longer and, making the affair into a game for the benefit of Nicolae and Elone, had us all strip and play in a shallow stream in order to cleanse our bodies and clothes. The water running down from the distant mountains where winter still held sway was ice cold, such as to be barely tolerable but we all, I am certain, felt better for the ablution.

Our clothes were badly soiled and ideally some form of detergent would have been welcome, but the worst excesses gave way to the combined efforts of running water and brute force and by the time I had completed my task, the three of us were once again respectable, though I longed for the luxury of a brush to tend our hair.

Fortunately, Elone had been well dressed by her parents in a heavy winter coat as well as a warm frock and camisole, and even underclothes, a luxury I had not experienced for a long time. Her family, I surmised, must have been one of relative wealth in the not so distant past, but I dared not question her upon the matter for fear of enkindling her interest in her missing parents.

For Nicolae and myself, our attire left much to be desired. Nicolae still wore my coat wrapped awkwardly around his body, for it was much too large for him. His own clothes, such as they were, had came reasonably clean in the stream and quickly dried. My sack-cloth frock was much the worse for wear, one shoulder having been ripped away by our rescuers when they tended my wound, and my dress now hung limply from the other shoulder, revealing the necklace and amulet Raisa had entrusted me with.

I was fortunate to have been donated the ragged blanket that I had been wrapped in during our brief time with the Resistance fighters, and which I now had slung about me as a makeshift jacket, whilst it served to cover us all as we lay huddled together of a night.

I was thankful, then, that the spring season was well advanced, the weather clement, with summer in prospect. Although I recognized progress would be slow, especially with two young children to conduct, I nonetheless estimated only a matter of days, perhaps a week at most, before we would arrive in Krakow, there to locate the camp whence Mama had been bound.

It was not the only misjudgement I would make.

~

By the third day the weather became unsettled and on the fourth it was clear our previous good fortune was at an end. The sky thus burdened by menacing storm clouds, their contents soon to be unleashed upon us, it became impossible even to hazard a guess at the sun's position and our direction quickly became a matter for conjecture. So low were the clouds hung and so mist-ridden the valleys that even the mountains were obscured, denying us all bearing.

The rain arrived not in drops but in torrents, with a driving wind that pierced our clothes and penetrated clean to our skin. Nor was shelter easily obtained, for the best we could do was to find a bush or small tree to huddle beneath, and the rain proved adept at attacking us from all directions, determined that no part of us should remain dry.

At first I made light of it, applauding the thunder, feigning awe at the lightning and rejoicing in the cool rain for the benefit of Nicolae and Elone, who joined in the game with relish. But as the downpour continue unabated hour after hour our bodies became chilled such that it became ever more difficult to distract my young charges from their condition.

Eventually the rain eased and we used the respite to move on, in the hope of locating a more substantial shelter, but wet clothes weighed down our spirits as well as our bodies.

What had a few days before been a refreshing and invigorating exercise, donning freshly washed clothes and allowing them to dry around us in the spring sun, now became a serious discomfort which, inevitably, Nicolae and Elone found intolerable, and they soon degenerated into querulous mood that drove me to despair.

Our sixth night was spent skulking beneath a lone tree that provided almost no shelter, in wet clothes that seemed to draw the cold winds mercilessly to them.

It was in such a state, with both children already reduced to tears, that the words I feared most were uttered, first by Nicolae, then quickly echoed by Elone. They were, of course, asking for their mothers and, cold, wet and exhausted myself, I was simply unable to provide them with the comfort and reassurance they needed at this time.

If they cried for their parents, my own tears were for them, and for much of the evening we wept together, until at last fatigue took its toll and sleep gained the upper hand. Helpless at this stage, I could only resolve in future to take shelter at the first sign of ill weather and not to venture on until the period of inclemency had passed, heedless of how long that policy might extend our journey.

Such planning did not resolve the immediate problem, however, and the next morning the children were no less distressed, for though the rain had stopped and the clouds lifted, the cold winds continued to blow down from the north, chilling our bodies, with no intimation of fairer weather to come.

As if this were not enough the ground had become a mire of mud and marsh, and as the mountains around us drew clouds to them and emptied their contents down upon us, so tiny streams turned to menacing torrents, not easily approached to drink from and quite impassable, obliging further detours that served only to confound further any sense of direction.

Thus burdened we were increasingly weak and hungry, our bodies beset by malnutrition, unable to counter the debilitating effect of climate and terrain. Fruits were sparse, for it was still early in the year, and of vegetation there was little beyond grass and rushes, and we were obliged to content ourselves with this jejune diet of cautiously selected berries and leaves for several days.

Only the thought of finding Mama in Krakow made possible my resolve to continue, for to turn back and head for Medgidia would have been far the easier option.

But on the ninth day the sun reappeared, a long lost friend against a cerulean sky, and with it our spirits lifted. We began the journey to Krakow once more, taking shelter at any sign of poor weather ahead. Occasionally, we would hear wolves howl in the distance, but we were fortunate not to be bothered with wild animals, although they were a constant, if unstated, fear at the back of my mind.

Rather it was we that posed nuisance to the local fauna, for Nicolae would take great delight in chasing any rabbit, hare or other small creature that ventured into sight, with the promise of returning with it for me to convert to a meal. I afforded myself some amusement in wondering how Nicolae would bring himself to kill such a creature in the unlikely event that he caught one, and this in turn begged the question how I would manage to cook the meat were he to succeed, for the making of fire without a sulphur-tipped match was quite beyond my abilities.

Our Polish benefactor Karol had anyway warned us most strongly against lighting fires, for fear of divulging our position to the enemy. I had at first been dismissive of his concerns, reasoning that for us the Nazis were not the enemy, for we were but lost children. But recalling how they had massacred the innocents on the train, women and children alike, I was forced to reconsider my position. It was chance, not the fact of our age, that had saved our lives that time.

With these thoughts in mind I lent consideration to our safety. If it had initially been my intention to foist ourselves upon the first people we came across, to seek food and directions, I now realised that, quite apart from the problem of language, we had no way of knowing how we would be received. What if they were sympathetic to the Nazi cause or otherwise ill-disposed to our well-being?

It was a problem I tried not to dwell upon, for there was no easy solution, hoping to postpone deliberation of the matter until circumstances dictated we confront it.

By chance that problem arose the very next day.

Chapter 29.

It was Elone's sharp eyes that described it; a flume of smoke above a distant woods, rising from the trees to dissipate against an azure sky.

It had been my intention to skirt the distant forest wherever possible, for I feared wolves or bears might lend us their unwanted attention if we ventured into its forbidding shadow.

By adhering to the highland slopes we could see in advance any threat to our well-being, man or beast, and take appropriate evasive action, I reasoned. Although thus far the only menace we had accosted was a curious mountain goat which ventured so close we could have reached out and touched its shaggy beard. In truth, I cannot say who was the more petrified, the children or I, but despite its forbidding horns the creature offered us no harm and duly went about its business indifferent to our fright.

But now I faced an altogether more serious dilemma: to approach the hamlet whose existence we had identified by its fumes, there to enlist their generosity to our best advantage, perhaps obtaining a meal and new directions; or to avoid it at all costs, for fear we would meet a dire fate.

Images of Nazi brutality were by now etched onto my mind, from the vicious jackboot assault upon young Elone at Bucharest station, to the machine-gun massacre we had so miraculously escaped.

We could not know if the inhabitants were of Nazi sympathies, or worst still that it was a Nazi occupied encampment of some sort...

Reason suggested the latter was unlikely, for if nescient of military strategy still I could fathom no purpose that an occupying force would require such an isolated settlement. I reasoned, too, such insularity favoured these sylvanian dwellers being native Poles with no sympathy for an invading, foreign army.

With such vague and competing thoughts in my mind I decided we should make a surreptitious approach and form a final judgement from a discreet distance. Of course, with my companions so young, lacking even the limited understanding of events my own twelve short years benefited me, I had of necessity to couch the proposal with a deal of fantasy.

Nicolae and Elone were busily chattering, seated on the rocky outcrop where, Elone having first seen the smoke rising from the distant forest, I had ordered we rest. I knew that, as the sun went down or the weather turned against us so would their spirits flag and thoughts of family once again dominate their young minds. It was, therefore, a matter of some urgency to take advantage of their currently cheerful disposition.

"Elone. Nicolae. Might I impose upon your time a moment?"

The children looked up as one and giggled together, as if sharing some private joke to which I was not to be privy. I sat down between them, drawing them to me with outstretched arms. "Huddle up, little ones. I have thought of a new game to play."

"A game?" Nicolae's eyes lit up. "What game, Anca?"

"A game of pretend," I said, suppressing a smile at Elone's wide-eyed delight.

"Yes! Let's play pretending!" she chuckled gleefully, her eyes brighter than I had seen them for several days, almost shining behind the muddy mask that hid her face. It was some days now since I had been bothered to encourage ablutions and now reminded of this fact I determined to have us all bathe at the next opportunity.

"Come on, Anca, what will we do?" Nicolae demanded, impatient for further detail. "What are the rules?"

I found myself thinking fast to produce a plan that would satisfy the children and at the same time achieve our end. "You see the flume of smoke yonder?"

All eyes turned to the forest distant.

"What we have to do is to explore the forest and secretly, invisibly, approach the fire and get warm."

"What is invisibly?" Nicolae asked.

"It means being invisible," Elone explained, leaving my little brother none the wiser. He looked to me for further clarification.

I lowered my voice conspiratorially and brought the two young heads close to mine. "It means without being seen," I said. "What we must do is to try and get as close as we can to the fire without being seen by the people there. We must pretend we are invisible, that no-one can see us, by keeping low to the ground, hiding behind bushes and trees and, all importantly, being as quiet as we possibly can."

The children were clearly enthralled by the proposition and I felt excitement rise in my breast as I explained, for in truth I was still a child myself, whatever the unwanted burdens of adulthood that had been thrust upon me in the form of my two charges.

Nicolae asked, "What if we are seen, Anca?"

I thought quickly. "Then you are out! Game over!"

Elone clapped her hands with delight. "Yes! Anca, I will be so invisible you will not be able to see me at all."

"And I will be so quiet you will think I am asleep," added Nicolae, not to be outdone.

"Do not do that, little one," I chided playfully. "When you are asleep you snore so loud that everyone can hear you."

At this feeble joke the children fell about laughing, playfully emulating snoring sounds and I took the opportunity to extract myself from their company and take account of our geography more carefully.

The forest was still some kilometres distant and the source of the smoke flume a distance further still into the woods. I studied the sky and estimated the time of day. It was gone noon and this concerned me, for I knew the forest would be dark and eerie even by daylight, and I had no wish to find ourselves lost within its murky depths after nightfall, when I reasoned hungry wild animals would be more disposed to roam.

Would it be better to stay outside the woods for the remainder of the day and venture into their depths at first light after we had rested, allowing us more time? From behind me I heard Nicolae and Elone cajoling, demanding the game commence and knew this was not an option. I had to take advantage of their enthusiasm immediately, for who knew how long it might last.

By tomorrow the weather might turn against us once more, dampening our spirits and weakening our bodies further. I knew also that, as we approached the source of the smoke flume that now held our attention, our very lives might depend upon the children's conviction that the game we were playing was of paramount importance.

With such considerations heavy on my mind and having determined an appropriate direction to reach the forest border, I gathered the children around me and we set off.

Chapter 30.

Whether my judgment of distance was at fault, or it was simply the fact of the many detours around rocky outcrops and torrential mountain streams that delayed us, it was already dusk by when we approached the woodland border, and my heart sank at the prospect of entering the forbidding forest by twilight.

I turned to find Nicolae and Elone crouched low behind a bush, for they had entered into the spirit of the game wholeheartedly as we had descended the steep slope towards the woods, on occasion even disappearing from my own view. In this I encouraged them with well-chosen words and vague promises of future reward, careful not to raise their hopes unduly.

Despite the many hours the descent had taken the children showed little sign of fatigue, for the game had invigorated their spirit and pushed from their mind such mundane matters as food and family. I knew it would be a mistake to call a halt and propose we rest until dawn, for to stop now would be a disappointment to them both and allow their thoughts to dwell on less cheerful concerns.

The distant sky was brooding and solemn, anticipating heavy rain, perhaps even storms to come, and suddenly the prospective shelter of the forest had its own appeal.

From our new position I could just make out the flume of smoke rising above the tree tops, still distant, yet too so very close. The air was already beginning to chill as the first clouds of the advancing storm obscured the sun, and the image of a warm fire, perhaps even a meal of some description, danced before my eyes.

Not since we had left Karol and his compatriots had we eaten a warm meal. Raw leaves, grasses and the occasional berry had been our staple diet for several days now, and the rigours of malnutrition were increasingly evident in the muddied features of Nicolae and Elone.

It was pointless to risk another night in the cold and rain when the prospect of warmth, food and shelter were just a short way distant. If we were found to be unwelcome, what did it matter if it were tonight or on the morrow?

I turned to the children and, raising my finger to my lips, whispered, "Here we go, little ones. Ever so quietly, ever so carefully." I led them cautiously into the trees, adding, "Stay close, for it will soon be dark."

In this my prescience was to prove unexpectedly accurate for no sooner had we crossed the divide between forest and hill than twilight was upon us, the coniferous canopy above shutting out even the ecru dusk that advanced menacingly across the mountains behind us.

At once Nicolae and Elone fell close to me, the distraction of the game suddenly of no consequence. It was not the mere fact of darkness itself that concerned them, for we had been alone in the dark many nights now. But rather the eerie, twilight silence of the forest invoked childhood images of fairy-tale demons and goblins, of witches and warlocks, and the fiercest of wolves and other ferociously hungry beasts.

I drew the children to me and hugged them both reassuringly, though in truth it was but an act, for my own fears were barely more controlled than theirs.

"Be not afraid, little ones," I said quietly, feigning conviction. "There is nothing here to harm us."

"I do not like it, Anca," Elone protested. "Let us go back, to the light."

Nicolae tugged at my arm, nodding his assent to Elone's suggestion. "It is scary here, Anca. I am frightened."

I put on a brave voice. "Don't be silly, Nicolae. Since when were you afraid of the dark? Have we not slept out in the darkness for many nights now?"

"This is a different dark, Anca."

I understood well what my brother meant, for the forest darkness was indeed different from the nights we had endured thus far. The evening sunlight barely penetrated the trees above and it was certain that, as nightfall came, the decrescent Moon's silvery gleam would not be adequate to the task, even without the gathering storm clouds to contend.

We had barely entered a few metres into the woods and already towering trunks loomed rampant from all directions, imposing and claustrophobic as an impenetrable wall. I could just make out the distant hill behind us and knew that, another few metres further, we would lose all sense of direction.

A rabbit ran out in front of us, as surprised to see us as we it. Startled by our presence it stopped before us, ears raised, bright eyes studying our motives.

Elone spotted it first and clapped her hand excitedly.

"Anca! Nicolae! Look!"

At her shout the timid creature turned on its heels and ran at lightning speed into the trees, disappearing from view.

I seized the opportunity, saying, "Look, children, the animals are more frightened of us than we of them. See, Elone, you scared the poor creature just by clapping!"

I clapped my hands loudly, daring any hidden fauna to challenge my authority. Of course no wild and hungry beast emerged from the darkness to do so. Somewhere above us a lone bird took flight, its wings beating the empty air loudly against the still silence of the forest.

Nicolae clapped his hands too.

There was only a resounding silence in reply, quite opposite to an echo, as if the trees soaked up the sound, capturing it by their very presence, determined never to let it go.

Elone clapped with Nicolae and the die was cast, our irrational fears for now set aside. Holding one another's hands we began to trace a path through the trees, treading cautiously over fallen branches and other pinaceous detritus that comprised the forest floor.

After a few minutes I turned and looked behind us, hoping for the reassurance of distant daylight of the slope we had just left, but the trees had closed in all around us and only the shallow prints of our footsteps betrayed the way we had come. Above us we could just make out the darkening sky, where clouds were gathering angrily in anticipation of the storm boding. I took some comfort from the dry forest floor, confident rain would not penetrate the canopy above.

What concerned me more was that already I was hazarding wild and ill-informed guesses as to our direction, hopes rapidly becoming prayers that the light of the fire we sought would shortly be visible before us.

My perfunctory invocations to a higher authority were to be disregarded, however, and we continued to wander aimlessly among the trees until darkness had encroached such that we could barely see one another, at which time I reluctantly conceded defeat and proposed to the children that we rest the night.

The proposal was better received than I anticipated, for they were by now exhausted, their tired minds occupied increasingly by their physical needs.

Thankfully our exploration of the forest had thus far brought no unwelcome encounters and the children's earlier concerns at the forest's eerie tranquillity had not yet cause to recrudesce.

I made out the nebulous form of a large, fallen tree near to us and announced this would be our camp for the night. It was no more or less comfortable than the resting places of recent evenings and I bolstered the children's appreciation of our new bed with the observation that it would be both warmer and drier than we had recently enjoyed.

We huddled together against the tree's trunk to sleep the night, enjoying one another's bodily warmth, taking comfort from physical contact. I talked quietly of our plans for the morning, of finding food of some sort and of meeting friendly people who might make us welcome, hoping to keep the children's minds from the reality of our plight: that we were lost in a dark and alien forest without food or water. Strangers in a strange land.

As I exhausted my list of hopes for the morrow, my own voice fell silent and I could hear the restful breathing of Nicolae and Elone. I felt better for knowing they, at least, had found escape in sleep. I hoped and prayed I could soon emulate their achievement but in this I was to prove ill-favoured.

Chapter 31.

I must have dozed a while at least, for I awoke with a start to the sound of rolling thunder from above. Dusk had given way to starless night, a fuliginous darkness that prevented me even seeing the heads of the children resting on my lap, though gentle hands assured me they were safe and well, sleeping despite the storm raging above the tree-tops.

If the canopy above us thrashed wildly and noisily in the storm, at ground level all was still. The air hardly moved and only the occasional splash of water penetrated the leafy roof to confirm the pouring rain above.

To say I was not scared would be untrue, but after a while I became blasé about the storm above, for we were cocooned by the forest from all but its boisterous sound and the all too frequent flash of lightning that would penetrate the very depth of the woods, illuminating all around us for an fleeting instant, then plunging everything again into the raven pitch of the forest's night.

At length the storm began to subside, the angle of lightning such that its fulgurations penetrated only the upper levels of our leafy canopy and the thunder rolled more distant, slowly parting our company. The wind eased too and the thrashing of the branches high above became a gentle sway. Still Nicolae and Elone slept, blissfully unaware of nature's ephemeral temper, and my own thoughts turned once more to join them.

Whether I succeeded a short while I cannot know, but I was next aware of the most blood-curdling of sounds and was in an instant bolt upright, my eyes wide with fear though the darkness was by now impenetrable.

At first I was as bewildered as I was frightened, for I had not been able to identify the sound, and I sat stone still, hardly daring to breathe, fearing what might come next.

For a fleeting moment my mind was filled with the tales of my early childhood, when Grandmama would scare Radu and I with haunting tales from Transylvania, of mythical creatures of the night that survived only by sucking the blood of the living. Instantly I struggled to shut my mind to these memories, remind myself I was twelve years old now, and that we had left our native mountains and their fanciful folklore far behind.

But in the still of the night, for the wind I now realised had deserted us along with the storm it brought, it was not easy to dismiss such childhood memories, and I silently cursed my grandmother's ability to bring to life the most improbable of fairy-tales. If only Radu were with us now.

Thoughts of my late brother were chased from my mind as the chill sound erupted through the night once more. This time wide awake, there was no mistaking its lupine origin, for the piercing howl of the wolf needed no introduction.

My blood ran cold, my body stiff and trembling. I gathered the stirring bodies of Nicolae and Elone to me, gently rocking them back to sleep, determined they should not share the fear that now held me tight in its grip.

Perhaps it was imagination, perhaps reality, but I now began to hear movement around us, though the inky darkness offered no chance of visual confirmation. My body shook with fear and, if laodicean of belief, still I began praying as I had not done in many years, begging deliverance from the evils that were even now surrounding us, preparing to seal our grisly fate.

The wolf howled again, still distant, but closer I was convinced, for its haunting call steered its way unerringly through the maze of trees to find its bourn: my very soul.

I shut my eyes tightly, as if this might aid in my defence, and clutched the children to me, determined that whatever the nature of our tormentor it would have to consume me first, to the very last bone of my frail body, before I would relinquish protection of my charges.

So disposed I sat and trembled through the night until eventually, whether in answer to my prayers or in response to fatigue I could not honestly say, I was delivered into blissful sleep.

Chapter 32.

I awoke to the touch of Elone's tiny hands on my shoulder, rocking me gently to release me from slumber, and I reluctantly opened tired eyes to the new day. The dark of night had been chased away by the morning sun and even beneath the green canopy the dawn's refreshed light penetrated to reveal the forest in all its splendour.

The thrusting trunks that stretched into the sky all around us were somehow diminished by the light of day, their menacing shadows held firmly at bay. The chimerical demons of the night had been banished to their lair and I took heart that the howling wolves that had prowled restlessly through the dark hours would now themselves be dormant.

"Anca! Anca! Look at Nicolae! He has new boots, Anca! Look!"

Elone's excited tones demanded my immediate attention and I followed her gaze to see my little brother hopping ungainly between the trees with what at first sight did indeed appear to be a gigantic boot about his foot.

My bemusement turned to amusement as he came closer and I realised he had found a hollow trunk among the debris of the forest floor perfectly suited to the size of his worn leather shoe and even now he was attempting an ungainly walk with the log adhered to his ankle.

I called out in encouragement, happy to see him smiling and laughing, conscious always that any preoccupation from our more immediate concerns of food and family were a welcome distraction. Elone rejoined Nicolae at play and I lay back, watching them, letting my body relax after an uncomfortable, all but sleepless night.

If the torment of the evening past was now only a memory, still I was determined I should not endure it another night and so gave thought immediately to finding the source of the fire we had identified the previous day. It was imperative that we achieve our aims soon, for the forest offered even less in the way of vegetation than the hills we had left behind. Only fungi seemed to grow in abundance here, and I knew not which was edible and which would prove deleterious, for none were familiar to me. To find the dwelling we sought, or else to exit the forest, was a matter for some urgency.

I ran my fingers through tangled hair in a futile attempt at emulating a comb and got to my feet, checking as always that Raisa's amulet was still safe around my neck. I brushed the detritus from my smock, pausing just briefly to entertain the otiose thought that it would benefit from some detergent.

"Nicolae! Elone! It's time to play our little game again. Remember?"

"Must we, Anca?" Nicolae protested with a sigh. He was thoroughly enjoying his new game, his trunked foot noisily crunching the twigs and leaves where he stood, and it seemed almost a shame to persist in my instruction.

"This is much more fun!" Elone declared, and I knew immediately that to call a halt to their game now would serve only to dampen their spirits and bring an unwanted solemnity to the day ahead.

Watching Elone dancing around my brother and clapping her hands, delighting in Nicolae's struggle to balance, I thought a moment, considering the options. Then, "Okay, children, you can play for just a little while. But we must make a start now. It is imperative you keep up, Nicolae, or I will take your new toy from you."

"I can keep up, Anca, look!"

Nicolae broke into a staggered run towards me. As he approached he lost balance and fell, laughing, into my arms. I took his weight and losing my balance we both crashed to the ground, rolling in the debris, laughing together. Elone needed no encouragement and joined us on the forest floor, falling carelessly among the detritus.

As our motion subsided we found ourselves as one supine among the dry leaves and fallen branches, looking up at the glimpses of blue sky through the green ceiling above. For a moment, as our laughter subsided, we fell silent, enjoying our mutual condition, all staring up to the heavens, each with our own private thoughts.

"Anca, the sun has crossed over," Elone announced suddenly, a hint of concern in her voice.

"What do you mean, Elone?" I asked, curious as to her worry. "How can the sun cross over?"

"It has," Elone insisted. "When you were asleep, earlier, when me and Nicolae first woke up, the sun was over there." She pointed into the sky a distance away.

I laughed quietly. "Nicolae and I, not me and Nicolae, fair one," I chided. A smile played on my lips. It was the kind of linguistic correction Papa would always be seizing upon, yet to make the point here in a distant Polish forest where such punctiliousness had no place seemed quite without reason.

I said, "It is nothing to worry about, Elone. The sun moves every day, rising in the east, setting in the west. It is just that normally we are not conscious of its motion." I paused, unsure whether my explanation meant anything to her inexperienced young mind, or indeed if I had myself correctly repeated the facts I had learned.

Then, as my own thoughts came together, I asked in urgent tone, "Elone, are you sure it was there before? How can you be certain?"

"Because I am, Anca," Elone assured me confidently. She looked about her and spied the fallen tree against which we had slept the night. "When I woke up this morning I was staring straight up and the sun was right above, like it was staring down as me. Now it's to one side, over there. See! So it must have moved!"

I received the news with mixed feelings, for it meant the day had advanced more than I first realised. That I had slept through the entire morning. But it was a reminder too that, so long as the sky was clear, we could still keep a sense of direction.

Thus emboldened we began to press our way between the maze of living trunks and decaying, fallen branches, I taking the lead, my eye now always toward the sun, with Nicolae and Elone close behind.

Chapter 33.

Progress was slow, for the irregularities of the forest floor did not make for easy passage, and I was relieved that Nicolae's speed was not too much impeded by his cumbersome attire. On the contrary the distraction of his walking with the log around his ankle kept both children amused, their constant laughter bringing a smile to my own face, and I resolved to let him continue his game so long as our pace remained unaffected.

At length we came to a trail of sorts, wending its way between the trees, and I examined it with a discerning eye. It was not a track trodden by humans, for the marks of small hoofed beasts were evident, but it was big enough to allow our passage and I resolved we follow it a while, for it would make for easier progress and might lead to a watering hole of some sort.

Elone's keen ears duly anticipated the sound of water and minutes later we came across a tiny stream running through the forest. It was but a small gully, ferrying a sparkling flow of rainfall from the mountains, but we were ecstatic at this discovery and fell as one upon its slight banks, cupping handfuls of the cool liquid to our lips, relishing the experience as parched throats were refreshed.

Sporadic flora had sprouted along the banks of the gully and, desperate for nourishment of any sort, I selected some coarse green leaves and we ate them quietly, obtaining some satisfaction from the motions of consumption, though they were tasteless and barely tolerable.

"Beggars cannot be choosers, little one," I chided Nicolae as he protested the offering. "Try and eat, for I know not when we will have another chance."

"You said we would meet the forest people and have real food," Nicolae sulked. "This isn't real food, Anca."

"It is all we have, Nicolae," Elone cautioned him. "It is better than nothing."

I smiled at Elone, for on such occasions she seemed mature beyond her years. Her blue eyes shone out from a dirt-ridden face, her once flowing blonde hair matted to her head, and I was overcome with the urge to mother her, to clean her hair, to wipe the filth from her face, and to expose her fair skin once more.

I cupped my hand and retrieved some water from the stream, applying it gently to her face. There was no protest as I ran wet hands across her cheeks smearing the mud away. At once I wished I had not, for without the grimy mask the true nature of her, of our, physical deterioration could be seen.

Her cheeks were sallow, her complexion pale and drawn. This was not the smiling face I remembered seeing on the train from Medgidia not so long ago. This was a face tormented by malnourishment and fatigue, bearing the scars of obscenities witnessed the like of which no-one, adult or child, should ever endure.

I felt tears forming ,and suddenly was overcome with emotion. Clasping Elone to me I began to cry. She looked into my eyes with a mixture of confusion and sympathy.

"Are you hurt, Anca? Where does it hurt? I will tend it for you."

"You are kind, Elone, but the pain is inside and cannot be reached." I let myself sob gently on her shoulder.

She put her arms around me and hugged me tight. "Never mind, Anca. Nicolae and I will look after you while you are hurting. Did I say it right this time?"

I managed a smile and nodded my head. I could see Nicolae looking on, unsure how to respond. I remembered how Papa used to chide him for crying, suggesting it was not a masculine emotion. It was one of the few things I disagreed with my father about, although I had never dared voice such reservations. I smiled at Nicolae, seeking to reassure him.

"It's okay, little one. I will be alright in a minute. Sometimes it helps to cry."

Nicolae looked aghast. "Girls are always crying," he announced, thankfully indifferent to his sister's sorrow. He hopped around in his wooden shoe. "I am going to explore some more, Anca. Elone, are you playing exploring with me?"

Elone shook her head. "I will stay with Anca while she hurts inside. Is that okay, Anca?"

I wiped away my tears with the back of my hand. "Thanks, Elone. Nicolae, do not go out of sight, do you understand? Just explore where I can see you."

"But Anca, that's not exploring, that's boring," he protested.

"You will do as you are bid, Nicolae," I said sternly.

They were the first sharp words of reprimand I had used since we had left Mama and they had an immediate impact, for Nicolae fell silent and, with an occasional glance in my direction to confirm my gaze, elected to play well within our presence.

I felt cool water on my cheeks and realised Elone was now applying herself to the task of cleaning my own face. I could see from her filthy fingers that I bore as much grime as she and I elected to lay back and let her continue her task, not so much from vanity as from the sheer enjoyment of her tender touch.

To my side I could hear the sound of running water as the impetuous stream traced the contours of the gully, oblivious to our presence. Above me birds sang and behind me I could hear Nicolae, refreshed by the cool water and what little of the leaves he had eaten, whooping playfully. I let my eyes slowly close, soothed by Elone's caressing fingers and the cool liquid against my skin.

Chapter 34.

When next I awoke it was dusk. I sat upright instantly, cursing beneath my breath to think I had allowed the remainder of the day to pass. I scanned the sky, but the sun had already sunk beyond the raised horizon of the forest and I knew that darkness could not be far behind.

"Nicolae? Elone?" I looked round, at first casually, then more urgently as their absence became apparent. "Nicolae! Elone!" My voice trembled as it rose, and I climbed to my feet, my legs unsteady after the long and unintended rest.

I was about to call again when I saw them, laying one against the other, fast asleep against a fallen trunk just a short way distant. I relaxed, a smile on my lips, relief to see them safe mingling with concern that they, too, were sleeping in the day.

If my first thought was that our oscitance might be the result of something we had eaten I quickly dismissed the concern, for I was awake now, with no ill-effect evident. Clearly nothing more than physical and emotional exhaustion had rendered us so tired. Even so I was annoyed that we had abused the daylight so.

I feared neither the children nor I would have the benefit of fatigue to help us sleep through the fast encroaching night. Should I wake the children now, that they might be tired later, or let them sleep on in the hope they would remain at rest until dawn? I elected to leave the young ones where they rested and use what little light remained to gather a few leaves for food and to make ourselves comfortable for the long night ahead.

Very soon it was too dark to manoeuvre safely and I presented myself at the side of my still slumbering companions and lay against them, to share our bodily warmth beneath our makeshift blanket as the evening air cooled.

Memories of the previous night's fearful imagery crowded my mind and I consoled myself with the prospect that, after so much rest, we would be fortified and able to take full advantage of the morrow's light to find the hamlet we sought amid the forest's depths. I shut my eyes against the forest's darkness and tried to dwell on pleasant thoughts.

Chapter 35.

I sat up with a start, to the piercing howl of a distant wolf, at once abruptly upright, unsure if I had fallen asleep and dreamt the sound or not.

A second, lingering howl ensued and I knew it was no dream.

I looked around me, trying to pierce the night with timid eyes, but only the sooty depths of the forest returned my gaze. Above me the sky was just visible, stars sparkling bright against what little I could see of the dark empyrean. There was no moon, or if there was the forest would not permit the lunar rays to penetrate its murky depths.

Another wolf howled, closer this time.

Much closer.

A shiver of fear ran down my spine and I instinctively reached out to comfort the children. As I did so a tiny hand clasped mine and Elone's voice said quietly, "Anca, I am scared."

I clasped her to my chest, wanting to reassure her, but my words lacked conviction. "There is nothing to be afraid of, Elone. It is just the creatures of the forest, going about their business. They will not bother us."

Elone clutched my fingers with her hand. "Do you promise, Anca?"

"I promise, Elone."

I was jealous now of the young child before me, for my assurances seemed quite enough to put her at ease, and even as I held her she drifted off to sleep again.

But for my part, sleep was no longer an option, fear my governing emotion and I was suddenly, acutely, aware of every sound the forest made.

In truth, of course, the background noise had always been there, but somehow my mind had until then been indifferent to it. Now every sound resounded, echoed, leapt out from the dark to declare its presence, and my whole body shook with fear.

I reached out to touch Elone and Nicolae, to reassure myself they had not been carried away by some wild beast of the night. Of course they had not and they slept on, oblivious to my trauma. But I could take no comfort from their indifference, for fear had taken hold of my mind, slowly prising my imagination from my control.

There were sounds all around me and I knew, I just knew, these were not mere products of an overactive mind, but the precursor of some real, some palpable evil that would shortly reveal itself.

The darkness was unrelenting and nothing could be seen, but I could hear the movement now, as this carnivorous monster of the forest approached, encircling us. It was coming closer, I was sure. I could hear the coarse, laboured breathing and I held my own breath, as if hoping it might not realise we were there.

A wolf? A bear? Some other hungry carnivore anxious to sate its appetite on human flesh? It was all I could do not to up and run, but I knew flight was impossible, even had I not the burden of my two young charges, miraculously still sleeping, oblivious to what might prove their last moments on this earth.

Suddenly it touched my foot and my body froze, fear in total control, even my vocal chords paralysed.

Yet somehow my sight was enhanced by my terror, and suddenly I could make out the form of the wild beast about to devour my leg. For a second all I could do was stare, open-mouthed.

Then, as realization dawned, my body began to shake, not this time with fear but with mirth, for the beast of the night that had caused me such dire anguish was nothing more than a harmless porcupine, on its way to the stream to slate its thirst.

As my laughter startled the poor creature it shuffled off into the night, never to be seen again, and I laughed all the more, until my sides ached and tears ran down my face. The act of laughter served to purge my mind of the fear that had gripped me and I knew, as my amusement subsided, that I would have a restful night hereafter. Even the intermittent howling of the distant wolves could not break my spirit now and I determined not to open my eyes again until the new dawn.

Chapter 36.

But I was not to see the dawn. I awoke to the urgent tugging of tiny hands at my face and in the darkness I could hear Nicolae's frightened voice. In an instant I was wide awake and clutching my little brother to my breast, suspecting he had awoken from a bad dream. But even as I offered comforting words the reason for his fear became apparent and I froze, sheer terror preventing further response.

The eyes that peered at me through the darkness were glowing, menacing eyes the like of which I had never seen before. The blood-curdling growl rolled from furled lips, exposing teeth that glinted even in the faint star-light. Yet all I could do was stare back, mesmerized by this dread spectre.

If I had never seen a real live wolf before, the fairy-tales of my childhood were replete with their menacing imagery and I needed no lesson in natural history to know our very lives now hung in the balance.

The beast patrolled before us, walking back and forth just metres distant, fulvous eyes never leaving us for a second, and I knew it was selecting which of us it would choose for its meal.

If fear paralysed my body my brain was working actively and I determined that if one of us must fall prey to the creature that the others might survive, then such was the burden I must assume.

Somehow I found strength to draw Nicolae to my side, edging his tiny form behind my own. Remembering Elone, I reached out blindly with my hands, my eyes never leaving those of the creature before us, until I found her arm and gently, slowly, began to bring her towards me. She stirred at my touch and murmured unheard words. I hushed her quietly, urging her to be calm and still, fearing she would panic and incite the wild beast to bring forward its inevitable assault.

Fear concentrated my senses and somehow my eyes were able to discern Elone's form in the darkness. I saw her turn to face the animal before us and as she did so her own eyes widened, her mouth opening to scream. It was an instant response for me to clasp my hand across her mouth to stifle the cry, drawing her terrified, shaking body to my own, forcing her behind me, where she clutched at Nicolae.

I could feel their defenceless young bodies tremor against my own and knew their fate rest solely on my ability to defend them.

I whispered, "Do not scream, children. Do not do anything. Just stay perfectly still."

Whether through fear or understanding they kept both still and quiet.

I pushed my hands behind me, offering the comfort of my touch, and felt them reciprocate. Before me the growling beast stopped in its tracks and turned to face us head on. I held my breath and was aware the children had done the same.

Elone began murmuring and I wanted to hush her, but hardly dared speak myself, for fear of inciting the beast further. I found the words, whispered from the side of my mouth.

"Elone, be silent. You will anger him."

But even as I spoke it dawned on me that Elone was speaking in Hebrew, and I realised from the ritual chant that she was at prayer. I found solace, somehow, that this small child, just nine years old, could be so composed in the face of danger and for an instant wished I too had some conviction in a higher being on whom to call, but the thought was quickly dismissed as the beast before us raised its head and let out a blood-curdling howl that clave the dark night like a sharpened axe.

I could feel the arms of the two children clutching at my waist, could hear their panicked breathing as they fought to hold back their screams, and I knew I must act.

I tried to visualize the ground on which we lay, hoping to recall some means of evading the canine predator that even now was preparing for its final assault. The trees, I knew, were tall, but lacking lower branches that might enable our escape upwards. Yet to contemplate out-running this creature of the night, even without the handicap of the forest's cloak, seemed futile.

As the wolf moved closer, looming minatorial from the darkness until I could smell its foetid breath and see the saliva drip from snarling fangs, I whispered to the children, "Prepare to run, little ones. I will count to three and then you must run. Run as fast as you can, both of you. Do not wait for me. I will try and distract the beast while you flee. I will catch you up later, do you understand? Nicolae? Elone? Please say you understand."

"We understand," Elone said. She clutched at my arm. "I will care for Nicolae, Anca. God will care for you."

I felt tears well in my eyes at her words, for she must have realised the sacrifice I intended, but there was no time for sentimentality. I knew that, if the two children were to have any chance at all of survival then I must act now.

I clutched at a fallen branch and whispered to the children, "I love you, Nicolae. You too, Elone." Then, "On the count of three. As fast as you possibly can. One. Two. Three! Go, Nicolae! Go, Elone!"

I jumped up, brandishing the fallen branch in my hands and took a step towards the creature, screaming "Come on, you foul beast, take me! Run, children, run!" I could hear their panicking steps as they made off into the darkness, but dared not turn to confirm their absence, nor even to ascertain their direction. There was anyway little point, for I knew I would not see them again.

My only thought was to hold this hideous creature at bay long enough that they might make their escape. The branch I held was of no consequence, for it could not possibly stave off the imminent attack, only offering the children precious seconds to get away.

I saw the wolf turn in the direction of the children, attracted by their commotion and, taking a deep breath, hurled myself forward at the beast, determined to have its undivided attention.

My bravado seemed to startle the creature, for it reared away, evidently unused to counter-assault, but the respite was short-lived. Seconds later the creature turned on me, moving closer, now undaunted by my feeble lunges with the branch.

The fear that had previously paralysed my movement now provided the adrenalin I needed to turn and run and I did so, pausing only to be sure I was heading away from the children.

As I left the clearing the starlight vanished and with it all semblance of visibility, but I ran on regardless, conscious only of the loping movements of the wolf behind me. I knew I could not possibly outrun the creature and guessed the beast was pacing me, waiting until I stumbled or fell exhausted to the floor before moving in for its final, ferocious attack.

I ploughed on through the darkness, somehow maintaining my balance, treading a precarious path through the undergrowth until I felt my breathing labour and knew I could not continue much further. I took comfort that the children must be far distant by now and found the energy to make a final spurt forward, reasoning that every step I managed would be a step towards their survival.

Then suddenly I was falling, as my feet became entangled in the debris of the forest floor. I hit the ground hard, knocking the air from my lungs, and turned to see the wolf lunging towards me. For what seemed like an eternity it hung in the air above me and I could see its every hideous feature in pornographic detail.

Then it was on me, my arms thrashing wildly in a feeble attempt to hold back its weight. Fulvous eyes shone like lanterns before me and I felt saliva splash across my face, blinding me. Puissant claws tore at my body and I screamed with pain.

The last thing I remember was the wolf's mephitic breath as the razor-sharp teeth pierced my skin.

Chapter 37.

Faint chimes sounded playfully across my senses and I lay still, taking pleasure from the refrain. Then, as memory activated and I recalled my last moments of consciousness, I sat up with a start, scorning the sharp pain that seared through my chest, staring about me into the blackness.

I could see nothing and for a few seconds presumed it must still be the dark night of the forest, but when I looked up to the sky not even a star shone.

The tinkle of bells chimed again, as if hanging in the wind, and I turned in the direction of the sound. I was aware of furnishing beneath me, this confirmed as investigating fingers reached down to touch a feather mattress. It was so soft, so gentle, after recent discomforts, that I was quite tempted to lay back to enjoy this sybaritic pleasure.

But immediately I thought of Nicolae and Elone I was upright again, calling their names, looking about me in bewilderment, trying desperately to bring a semblance of order to a confused mind.

There was no answer to my cry, only the faint chimes responding to my call. I reached down again to the mattress, to confirm its existence, that it was not a figment of my overwrought imagination.

It was not.

I looked about me again. The air was redolent with vernal flowers but still the darkness was pervasive. I called out the children's names once more.

No answer.

Suddenly there was a noise before me, as if a door opening. I followed the direction of the sound but saw nothing. A voice, a woman's voice, spoke to me in a tongue I did not recognize, though the tone was soft, gentle. Still I saw nothing. The thought struck me suddenly, that I was blind, and I reached instinctively to my eyes, probing fingers denied contact by a cloth restraint.

As I began in panic to tug at the material, warm hands gently gripped my wrists, drawing them down to my side. Demulcent tones gave meaning to a language otherwise unfamiliar and I offered no resistance. I demanded, "Please, who are you? Where are Nicolae and Elone? Are they safe?" My questions gushed out, each one begun without pause for an answer to the previous, but all I received in reply were soothing words evidently urging me to rest.

I importuned my benefactress indifferently. "Nicolae, my brother? And Elone? Are they safe?"

It was obvious I was not understood, but still I persisted in my enquiry, for the welfare of the children was my only concern just now. If obvious enough I had by some miracle survived the wolf's attack in the forest, the fate of my brother and charge remained a mystery, and one I could not conceive of rest before resolving.

I tried to sit up again, but the gentle hands were guiding me back, laying me against the feather mattress. I felt a receptacle at my lips and realised I was being offered water. I gulped down a few mouthfuls, thankful for the refreshment, then shook my head to indicate I could take no more. As the clay bowl was moved away I asked again, "Nicolae? Elone? I must know."

The reply made no more sense to me than my questions to her and I realised my benefactress was stepping away. I wanted her to stay, to explain, to give me hope, but knew words were pointless just now. I heard the door open and close and I was alone again, only the aeolian chimes breaking the silence.

I probed the bandage across my eyes with cautious fingers, then lay back, pondering my plight. Logic dictated I must be in the tiny hamlet in the forest that we had identified from afar some days prior. That much seemed reasonable, for only those very inhabitants would surely have been on hand to find me.

Working things through my mind it was sensible too to suppose the language my benefactress spoke was Polish, though I could not be sure, for I had no prior claim to familiarity with its tones.

Extrapolating further, I reasoned she or they must have found me after the wolf had left me for dead, bringing me back to their home and tending my wounds.

My wounds.

I became conscious of the pain in my chest once more and reached a hand to feel the damage. My chest too was heavily bandaged and I quickly traced my body with my fingers to ascertain what other lesions I had received, but remarkably I appeared to have incurred no further injury.

I took further solace on finding Raisa's amulet still safe about my neck.

Conscious now of a curious fragrance emanating from the liniment around my torso I guessed I had been tended with some bucolic poultice and this in turn gave me reassurance that I, at least, was in safe hands.

But with that thought my attention turned once more to the plight of my brother Nicolae and the dear child Elone.

Had my survival been at their cost?

Had the wolf left me to track them down instead?

Had they perhaps succumbed to another member of the foul beast's pack?

My thoughts were myriad and sombre, fearing the worst. Even had they escaped the canine predators that night, what chance two children so young to fend for themselves in the forest? If they were indeed alive still, how much longer could they maintain such a disposition? Thus burdened with guilt I had no choice but to take immediate action.

I swung my legs across from the mattress to find the floor below and hesitantly tried to stand. My body was weak, but I managed to hold myself steady. I could hear the wind chimes tinkle to my left and knew therefore that the doorway was to my fore. But without sight I hesitated to take a step, fearful that I might stumble at some obstacle and incur further injury.

Even as I contemplated my options the door opened and an angry voice assailed my ears. Hands were upon me in seconds, guiding me gently but firmly back to my mattress. My benefactress spoke to me at length, though she must surely have known I could not understand her words, using the pressure of her hands to indicate I must stay put, and I resigned myself to the torture of uncertainty.

Suddenly my heart leapt as the unmistakeable shrill of Nicolae's voice called my name and seconds later I felt his body lunge against mine, tiny arms wrapping themselves tight around my neck, accompanied by a gabble of chatter so rapid I could make no sense of it.

Overcome with relief to find my little brother safe I could barely manage a composed response myself and for perhaps several minutes I managed only a mixture of laughter and tears as I struggled to tolerate the pain in my chest, to enjoy my sibling's body against mine.

Eventually Nicolae fell quiet, exhausted by his eager salutation, and I clutched him tightly, braving the pain, wondering if I dared voice the question poised on my lips.

I had to know.

I asked quietly, "Nicolae, is Elone with you?"

Chapter 38.

I felt his hands grip mine and knew instantly that she was not.

I felt him shake his head and his body heave as he struggled with the words.

"She is gone, Anca. Nobody knows where."

I fought back the tears, but the resistance was futile. Already weakened, I had no control over my emotions and wept openly, until I could feel the bandage against my eyes reach saturation and salty tears began to drip down my cheek. I felt the firm hand of my benefactress against my shoulder, offering incomprehensible but comforting words.

Composing myself with difficulty I said, "Little one, do you know where we are? Who is this woman that aids us so?"

Nicolae raised his head from my chest. "I do not know, Anca. She is a lady. There is a man, too, but they cannot speak properly. Their words make no sense. I tried to tell them about Elone, but they would not listen."

I traced Nicolae's face with my fingers. "We are in a different land, Nicolae. It is not that they will not listen, just that they do not understand. They speak a different language. Polish, I suspect."

I paused, realising my explanation was beyond Nicolae's comprehension.

I asked, "Nicolae, are we still in the forest? Are we in the dwelling we sought?"

"I think so, Anca." I felt his fingers near my eyes. "Why are your eyes bandaged?"

I took his hand in mine, guiding it away. "My eyes need to rest, Nicolae, that is all. How about you, little one? Are you harmed in any way?"

"No, Anca. The man and the lady looked after me when they found me. I have had a bath and lots to eat, while you have been asleep."

"That is good to hear. Have I been asleep long, Nicole?"

"Two days."

"Two days?"

Was this an accurate statement or a misconception of time's passing by my little brother? I had no way of knowing. But if it were true then there could be scant hope for Elone, lost still in the forest.

I fought back tears and clutching my brother's arms said, "Nicolae, the people who helped us. Are there just the two of them?"

"Yes, Anca."

"How did they find you?"

"I found them, Anca."

"You found them? Explain, little one."

Nicolae paused, as if gathering his thoughts, mentally rehearsing his response.

He said at last, "It was after you told us to run, Anca. Do you remember? The big dog was there, then you told us to run and me and Elone both raced as fast as we could. We ran and ran until we heard you scream and then we stopped, frightened, and heard a really loud bang. We did not know what it was, Anca, but Elone said she would go and see. She told me to stay where I was, that she would come back for me..."

His voice trailed. I took his hand, stroking his wrist, wishing I could see his face.

"What happened then, little one?"

"She never came back for me, Anca. I waited for ages and ages, truly I did, but she never came. I was so frightened on my own that I decided to go to her."

"But you could not find her."

"No, she was nowhere, Anca. I just kept walking, hoping I would find you or she. Then I saw this house and went to the door. The lady answered and took me in and there you were, lying on the floor in front of the fire, covered in blood. I ran to you, but the lady would not let me hold you. She would not listen to me or speak properly to me or anything."

"That is okay, Nicolae. Do not hold it against them, for they are kindly people. The lady, she is still here with us now?"

"She is there, Anca." He took my hand and guided it to my benefactress, evidently sitting just beside me, perhaps trying to make sense of our conversation.

I held my hand out and felt rugose fingers slip into my palm.

I said slowly, as if hoping I might be understood better for it, "My name is Anca." I released her hand and put my palm to my heart. "Anca. Anca." I found Nicolae's head and patting it said, "This is my brother, Nicolae. Nicolae. Nicolae."

"Nicolae," the woman repeated. "Nicolae. Anca." She took my hand and held my palm against her face. "Izabella," she said. "Izabella."

"Hello, Izabella. I am so very pleased to meet you. Nicolae, the lady's name is Izabella."

"How can you know, Anca? How can you know what she says?"

"Be assured, little one, we will manage."

I turned to my benefactress again and held my hand to her, then to Nicolae and myself, saying, "Izabella. Nicolae. Anca." I moved my hands together and gestured a human form, flattening my palm to indicate Nicolae's height.

"Elone? Izabella, please, there is another child. Elone. Elone. Nicolae, say it too. Elone."

"Elone. Elone," Nicolae repeated.

There was silence, as if digesting this message, then from Izabella, "Elone?"

I nodded, "Yes, Elone. She is nine years old, but small like Nicolae. She was in the forest with..."

I stopped, remembering I was not being understood, that only the simplest of communications were appropriate.

"Elone," I said, using my hands to illustrate an imaginary child in the air. "Elone."

Suddenly I felt Izabella's hands against my cheeks as she stood before me. She said something quietly, eased me to a prostrate position, speaking again. I guessed it was for us to remain still while she left us, and I could only hope she had understood that a further child was still in the forest somewhere.

As the door closed, Nicolae said, "Where is the lady going, Anca?"

My answer was immediate and confident. "To fetch Elone, little one. Be patient. She will be here with us soon."

I prayed my intuition would not prove me a liar.

I felt Nicolae leave my side and run across the room. "I can see the lady, Anca," he said excitedly. "She is talking to the man."

"Her name is Izabella, Nicolae," I chided quietly. "I would think the man must be her husband. No doubt we will learn his name in due course. What is he doing?"

"He was chopping wood, Anca, but now he is coming back to the house. But the lady, Izabella, she is staying outside."

"Keep talking, Nicolae. For the next few days, at least, you must be my eyes. You will have to tell me all the things I cannot see. Will you do that for me, little one?"

"I will try, Anca."

"So what can you see, Nicolae? Tell me what you see."

"Just the forest, Anca. There is a garden, where the lady, where Izabella, is standing, and then the forest. And here comes the man again. Anca, he has a gun. A huge gun! Why has he — Oh! Oh, Anca! Anca!"

I sat up, his excited tones demanding my attention. "Nicolae, what is it?"

"The dog, Anca! The big dog! I can see it!"

My heart missed a beat and I was struggling to my feet. "Nicolae, shout to Izabella quickly! It is a wolf! Warn her!"

Nicolae's laughter in response was at once disconcerting and reassuring. "But Anca, it has no head!"

"No head?"

"Honestly, Anca! It has been chopped clean off! I can see it on the ground near the body. And lots of blood! Lots!"

I could not help but smile at this macabre report, for there was no prospect of sympathy for the beast that had so nearly claimed my very life. It was, of course, but supposition that this was indeed the same creature, but all reason suggested it must be.

Nicolae's earlier story began to make sense in my mind now. Izabella's husband must have been in the forest at the time of our attack and came across the wolf even as it set about me. Presumably armed with the same gun Nicolae had just seen, the man had been able to finish the creature there and then, bringing both the beast and its victim to his home, the one to behead, the other to tend her injuries. Nicolae must have presented himself at their door soon after. That much I could fathom.

But of Elone, I could only hope and pray that she was still safe and would soon be found. For now, exhausted by my ordeal and thankful at least to have Nicolae with me, I allowed myself to be lulled by the aeolian chimes and the tranquil susurration of the forest.

Chapter 39.

I awoke to the sound of birds singing and for a moment I was back in my own bedroom in far away Medgidia, listening to the dawn chorus that greeted me each morning before Mama would call me to prepare for school.

From the birds' song I guessed it must be dawn now and that I had therefore slept soundly through the night. Certainly I felt better for it. But as I tried to open my eyes and felt the cloth restraint, my plight came rushing to mind. At once I was concerned for the children.

I called out, "Nicolae? Are you there, little one? Nicolae?"

After a brief pause I heard the door open and Izabella's voice greeted me with a salutation in her own tongue. I heard her approach and felt her peck a greeting kiss on my cheek, just as Mama used to do. I reached out and, finding her hand, clutched it tightly, knowing words were pointless at this stage.

She spoke to me softly, guiding me with her hands to indicate her intent. I was lifted to a sitting position and my legs drawn to the floor. I guessed she wanted me to try and stand and I resolved to put all my energy to that purpose. The long rest had indeed done me good, for I found the task not too difficult, though I needed to lean against my benefactress for support.

She continued to speak to me, though she surely knew her words were not understood, and began to guide me forward. I heard the door open and was led through into the next room. I could hear water splashing and turned in that direction. The sound of children laughing. I held my breath, not daring even to hope.

Izabella called out something and I heard the water foam as bodies turned.

"Anca! Anca!"

My arms were outstretched and tears streaming even before her tiny body reached me. As Elone leapt up at me I felt Izabella steady me from behind and my arms wrapped around the child's soaking body, clasping her to me heedless of the pain in my chest the action wrought.

I heard Nicolae running towards me too, shouting my name, and braced myself for his arrival, unable to muster words to express my feelings.

If learning that Nicolae was safe the previous day had been emotionally draining, to have both Nicolae and Elone together now was beyond compare.

I felt Nicolae clambering upon me, his wet body soaking my clothes, and for a moment could do nothing but stand and cry, supported by Izabella by my side, as I was assailed by their eager greetings.

The children gabbled simultaneously, each telling their own tale, but I was too overcome with emotion to listen. At length I heard Izabella's voice cajoling them to climb down and felt the burden lift as she prised first one child, then the other, from around my neck. I heard each one splash into water and Nicolae shout out, "Anca, we are having a bath! Come watch us!"

Of course I could not see them, though the splashing water and their naked, wet bodies had already apprised me of their activity.

"I am coming, children," I said, and tentatively stepped toward the commotion.

I felt Izabella take my arm and guide me to their location. She eased me onto my knees and I gripped the sides of an iron tub to gain my bearings. One of the children playfully splashed me with water and received what by tone was clearly a mild rebuke from Izabella.

"Anca, what has happened to your eyes?" Elone demanded. "Are you blind?"

"Of course not, Elone," I said, though the suggestion caught my breath, for I had not until then considered the possibility my disability might be permanent. I dismissed the thought. "Izabella will tell me when I can take the bandage off."

"You understand her, Anca? But she does not speak Romanian."

"Nor I Polish, Elone, but we can understand each other if we try. Now little friend, tell me what happened? How did you come to be here? I cannot begin to express how worried I was about you."

"And I you, Anca." She took my hand, clutching it tightly. "I thought I should never see you and Nicolae again."

I could imagine her earnest face as she spoke, and not for the first time was thankful for her friendship. If her tender nine years told against her in terms of experience of life, still she was a friend in a way I could not conceive of considering my beloved little brother.

"How did they find you, Elone? Did you come to any harm?"

"None, Anca. The man found me, in the forest. I remembered what you had taught us, Anca, that he might be a soldier, a Nazi, and I hid from him, but my camouflage was poor for he saw me hiding and shouted out to me. He called my name, Anca, so I knew he must have found you and Nicolae already."

I smiled to acknowledge her story. "Go on."

"He is a nice man, Anca. He brought me home, here, and that is when I met Nicolae again. He told me immediately that you were safe, but they would not let us see you. I think they wanted you to rest. They fed us both, and this morning they prepared us this bath first thing. Then suddenly we turned and there you were!"

Elone paused, gathering her thoughts, then, "Oh, Anca, please promise you will never let us be parted ever again. I was so frightened out there all on my own."

I replied with quiet assurance. "I promise, Elone. I promise."

Chapter 40.

For six long months keeping that promise was to prove a simple task, for that entire time we spent as guests of Izabella and her husband, Wojciech.

Certainly it was not our intention to stay so long. If the first week was unavoidable, until my bandages were removed and my sight restored, that weeks became months was very much at the insistence of our hosts.

I had correctly surmised they were but peasants eking out an exiguous subsistence from the forest, and though they spoke no language beyond their native Polish the problem of communication proved quickly surmountable. Even in the first week we began to pick up occasional words, the better to make ourselves understood, and as the months passed all three of us began to develop a command of the language, perhaps Elone most of all.

Spring turned to summer almost unrealised in the sylvanian cocoon of the forest's depths, and by the time autumn beckoned we were, if far from fluent, certainly competent to converse of simple subjects with our hosts.

In the latter months of our stay I was to learn much about our situation. My early fear that we might be turned over to the Nazis, especially when Elone's Jewish background became known, was quickly banished, for Izabella and Wojciech were among the kindest people one could wish to meet, devoted selflessly to our welfare.

If their lifestyle was unfamiliar to us, both for its pastoral nature and its senescence, still we fell quickly into the diurnal routine of forest life.

The first month was one spent resting and re-nourishing our bodies, building up our strength after our harrowing ordeal, but once my bandages were removed I was able to help Wojciech about the forest and later even to accompany him to a nearby town where he bartered chopped wood and mushrooms for other goods.

Elone too made herself helpful, assisting Izabella about the house, always to be seen besom in hand, and even taking on a maternal role to my little brother, caring for him when I was unable to.

Somehow this remarkable child played the roles of juvenile friend and substitute mother simultaneously, at once a laughing, giggling little girl playing silly games with Nicolae, yet also tending his needs and caring for him in a manner that entirely belied her years and left me eternally indebted to her.

As my command of the language developed, I began to piece together the nature of our Polish hosts' lifestyle, and soon came to realise it was not quite the epitome of rustic innocence it first appeared.

Early into our stay Nicolae had, in the course of a game of hide and seek with Elone, stumbled across a cache of weaponry that stood in stark contrast with the peasant shotgun Wojciech carried about the forest to procure our meals and fend off wild beasts.

I urged the children to ignore their find and play elsewhere, but my suspicions were now aroused and for several weeks I was fearful that my first impressions were in error and that our hosts were indeed Nazi sympathizers, perhaps awaiting the opportunity to turn us over to the authorities for some indecent reward.

But in the second month of our stay all was to be explained and my mind put at rest.

We woke one morning to find new guests, one a badly wounded soldier wearing a uniform instantly recognisable by the hammer and sickle insignia as Russian. The others were clearly Polish partisans, dressed and armed much as those who had dragged us from the train after the derailment, and though at this stage my Polish was not up to conversation it became apparent Izabella and Wojciech were fierce patriots to their country, ready to risk their life to take in and tend the needs of wounded men leading the fight against the Nazi occupation.

The Russian spoke no Romanian but was competent in Polish and so able to inform our hosts of the latest developments in the war, which in due course Izabella would impart to me. I was heartened to learn advances were being made on both the eastern and western fronts, and that the wounded Russian believed the war to have reached a turning point.

That said, there was no hope of a cessation of hostilities in the near future and the fate of the occupied countries, Poland and my native Romania among them, hung in the balance.

I was fired with inspiration by this news, wishing I could do something constructive to help, but knew my immediate duty was to my little brother and Elone, and the reuniting of our families.

In the last month of our stay, in my broken Polish, I put my concerns to Izabella and Wojciech as we sat around a log fire one autumn evening, soon after the younger children had retired for the night.

Chapter 41.

"Please do not be offended," I began hesitantly, "when I say we must leave soon. "

They exchanged glances but said nothing.

"Your hospitality has been unsurpassable and, I assure you, I could happily spend the remainder of the war here as your guests for I, and I know this to be true of the children too, have come to regard you as family."

I crossed and took the hands of Izabella and Wojciech, struggling to find words difficult enough in my own language, and almost impossible to express in what little Polish I had learned.

"Izabella, you have been as a mother to me these past months. And you, Wojciech, like a father. To all three of us. But our real mother, mine and Nicolae's, and the parents of Elone, may still yet be alive. As I have explained previously, they were bound for a resettlement camp somewhere beyond Krakow. That much I know. Please understand we cannot rest until we have ascertained their fate, for better or worse."

Izabella took my hand with both hers, offering reassurance. "We understand, Anca. Of course you must seek your family, though in all honesty we must warn you to expect the worse, for only then can you avoid bitter disappointment."

Tears welled in her eyes as she spoke. "We will be sorry to see you leave, for your presence here has brought us much joy, Anca. But we will not stand in your way."

I was relieved to hear this, for I anticipated they would object.

"We have not mentioned this before, Anca, but now perhaps the time is right. We had a son, once, Wojciech and I. Krzystof, his name." She struggled to express her thoughts and I listened patiently.

"He was killed in battle in the early months of occupation, some years ago now, even as his wife Mila lay enceinte with what would have been our grandchild." My host struggled with the words. "She too was a Jew, Anca, like your friend Elone. She... That is..."

Izabella was overcome with emotion and I sat at her side without hesitation, to offer comfort and succour. As I warmly hugged her, Wojciech took up her story.

"After Krzystof death, Anca, his wife Mila, then living in Krakow, was moved into a ghetto, a Jewish ghetto, in the city. All the Jews were moved there, you understand, regardless of nationality or social standing. By their religion they were branded, judged and sentenced." He paused, and I realised he was struggling to control his own emotions.

One arm still around Izabella, I reached a hand to his, urging him to continue. "What happened to her, Wojciech?"

"We do not know even if she is still alive, Anca. We heard that the ghetto had been liquidated, and that those who survived had been sent on to labour camps, just like your mother and Elone's parents. Mila was sent to a place called Treblinka, in the north-east of our country. We know at least that she arrived there, for we received a message confirming her admission. That was more than a year ago, since when we have heard nothing. No news of her, or our grandchild."

"But Wojciech," I said, "if she arrived at the labour camp then surely she must be safe and well? Surely you anticipate meeting her again once the war is over?"

At this suggestion Izabella clutched me to her and began to cry again. Wojciech turned from my mystified gaze, unwilling to meet my eyes, and I knew there was more.

I demanded, "Wojciech? What is it? Is there something you are not telling me?"

It seemed an eternity before he answered. "Anca, you are so young. There are some things perhaps best left unsaid, unsuited to a child's ears."

"I am twelve years old, Wojciech. Almost a teenager. Please, do not treat me as you would Nicolae or Elone."

Wojciech considered my request. "It is just rumour, Anca, not fact. In any war, my child, truth is the first casualty. I cannot tell you things I do not know to be true."

"Please, if there is something I ought to know, if it might have a bearing on my mother's fate, then you must tell me."

Wojciech shook his head. "I will not fill your head with gossip, child." He paused, deep in thought, then, "Anca, we understand that you must go. We will not stand in your way, for you are of independent mind and we know our protests would be futile. But please, leave the two children with us. Let us care for them for you while you go in search of your mother."

I was shaking my head before even he had completed the sentence, not willing even to consider the option.

"No, Wojciech, I cannot do that. Your offer is greatly appreciated, but Nicolae is my brother and we will not be parted. I promised Mama, and Papa before that, I would care for him and so I must, no matter what. And Elone..."

I implored with them with my eyes not to contest what I was about to say.

"Elone is as a sister to me now, though I have known her only a few months. It is incumbent on me to care for her as my own. Please, Wojciech, please, Izabella, try to understand I cannot relinquish my duty to them. Please do not try to stop us leaving, all three of us."

Izabella, her voice wrought with emotion, said, "That we will not do, Anca. We understand your plight, for as Wojciech explained, we were faced with a similar dilemma. If our years were fewer and our bodies more able then no doubt we would have gone to Krakow to try bring Mila back with us. But we were ignorant then. How could we possibly know the tragic way events would unfold?"

I nodded my understanding.

"Now we do our bit, as you have witnessed, Anca. It is as much as we can do. I am sure you realise we risk our very lives to receive partisans and wounded soldiers here. That is our own small contribution to this fight against tyranny."

She squeezed my hand reassuringly. "Yours will take a different form, Anca, for I know you are as dedicated to that cause as we are. But that in the first instance the search for your respective families must be paramount."

She paused, selecting her next words carefully. "No, Anca, we will not try to stop you leaving, not you or the children, if that is your will. You are brave beyond your years, my child. Of course you must take Nicolae with you, and if you are to look after your brother properly then you will need the able assistance of Elone, for she is a blessed child, as you must realise. You are better off with her than without, of that I am convinced."

She turned to Wojciech and whispered in quiet and rapid Polish such that I could not understand, before turning back to me.

"Anca, if you must leave, then please let us assist your journey in this way. Wojciech has a brother, Henryk, resident still in Krakow. He is a good man, Anca, and may be able to assist you, if only to point you in the right direction as you go about your mission. If you go to him he will help you, of that I am confident."

I nodded my appreciation. "Thank you. Both of you. Krakow is indeed our destination, for I know the train at Bucharest was bound that far. Is it distant, this town, Krakow?"

Wojciech said quietly, "A long way, Anca, but we will see you get there safely. Henryk will make you welcome for a few days while you establish the true nature of your task. Then... Then, Anca, hopefully you will realise the futility of your endeavour and return to us here in the forest until the war is over, after which perhaps we will all be reunited with our surviving families."

Chapter 42.

Wojciech was true to his word in doing everything possible to prepare us for our journey. In particular he coached us in Polish phrases which we might find especially helpful.

Izabella devoted much time to Elone, who was by now at least as competent in the language as I, and stressed repeatedly that she should never recite her Talmud incantations in public. She should be proud always of her Jewish heritage, Izabella told Elone, but for now she must pretend she was indifferent to religion, or at best of Catholic stock.

Having seen how the Jews had been treated at Bucharest station I could only support Izabella in promoting this deception, although it went against everything Papa had taught me about standing up for one's beliefs.

It was agreed we would depart when Wojciech next made his foray into town with his cartload of logs and forest wares. That way we could ride into town without drawing undue attention to ourselves. He would show us to the railway station and purchase us tickets for the journey to Krakow.

I protested that we could not presume upon what little money he had, for we had already partaken for many months of their worldly goods, eating deep into their winter reserves. But Wojciech would have none of this.

If we were intent on pursuing our course of action, he said, we would do so with every assistance he and his wife could muster. There was little point arguing, for his mind was set, and in truth we needed every advantage we could obtain, for we were strangers in a strange land and our task was onerous enough without the additional burden of having to make our own way to Krakow.

I promised them we would return one day and repay them their kindness, though these were but empty words, for I knew it implausible we would ever meet again.

When the day of our departure arrived we bathed early, relishing what might be our last hot bath for some while, and were fed a particularly splendid breakfast to fortify us for the long journey ahead.

During our stay Izabella had made us new clothes and somehow had obtained shoes to fit us, for which we would be forever indebted. We were provided with a bag filled to the brim with cakes and oatmeal bread, which we were advised to consume sparingly, less the journey to Krakow be delayed in any way.

At mid-morning, as I struggled to find the parting words to express our gratitude for their kindness, we each kissed Izabella goodbye and mounted the loaded cart. Tears flowed freely as we followed the track into the forest and out of sight of our friend.

The children found the ride uncomfortable after so many months cushioned from life's harsh realities, but it was soon over, for we arrived in town in little more than an hour and spent midday in the market place watching as Wojciech haggled for the best return on his wares. German soldiers were in evidence, but not in great numbers, and we did not see any hated SS men.

As the village clock struck the second hour of noon Wojciech gathered us together and led us in silence through the market place to a ramshackle station, running to little more than a ticket office and guard's quarters beside rusting rails.

He beckoned for us to wait quietly and disappeared into the office, to return shortly with three tickets to Krakow. He handed these to me along with a sealed envelope which he cautioned me to entrust to no-one. It was addressed to his brother Henryk, his home details scrawled onto the face of the envelope. On the back he had drawn a rough map of how to find the address from Krakow station.

"Obviously we have no way of warning him of your arrival, Anca, and he will be most surprised, and not a little suspicious, to find three children so young descending upon his home unannounced, so it is imperative you do not lose this letter of explanation."

I assured him it would be kept safe about my person.

"Once he realises you are friends of ours Henryk will not hesitate to make you welcome," he continued. "But I stress only for a few days at most. Please do not let yourself think he can extend his hospitality further than that, for the Nazis are in occupation of Krakow and you will place both him and yourselves at risk by exceeding your welcome. Do I make myself clear, Anca?"

I nodded, sobered by this warning. Whilst in the secure comfort of Wojciech's home it had been easy enough to envisage setting off again on our journey. But now, faced with the grim reality, the prospect was daunting.

Wojciech saw my hesitation.

"It is not too late to change your mind, Anca. You are welcome to return with me now. Perhaps just for the winter? Perhaps it would be better to wait until the spring to travel?"

I took his hand, anxious to demonstrate my gratitude. "Thank you, Wojciech, but no thank you. We must do what we must do. We will remember you and Izabella always, that much I promise. Goodbye, Wojciech."

I leant up and kissed him on the cheek. He bent down and allowed Elone and Nicolae to do the same.

"Goodbye, children, and good luck. I will go now, for to be seen with you when the train arrives might be unhelpful to us both."

He ushered us towards the gate. "Go now, and be brave, my friends. Henryk will see you right."

With those words he turned and left us, three children alone in a town we did not even know the name of, waiting, anxious, for the train to Krakow.

Chapter 43.

If once the awesome sight of a steam locomotive heaving into view had brought a rush of intense excitement, now it awakened only bitter memories. Elone held my hand tight, while even Nicolae was subdued as the mechanical behemoth advanced upon us, and I knew we were all thinking the same thoughts. Our laden silence required no explanation.

The engine ground to a shuddering halt and a blast of steam issued forth from between the filthy wheels, barely missing us, but we seemed hardly to notice.

I looked around the station for confirmation that the train was bound for Warsaw, where Wojciech had told us we must change trains to complete our journey. A guard was dutifully chalking the relevant information onto a weathered board. No passengers alighted and I noted with disinterest that we were the only three people to embark.

We selected our seats carefully, opting for an empty centre carriage. A hiss of steam could be heard as the engine generated power and suddenly the wheels screamed against unforgiving rails and we lurched backwards as the carriages groaned into motion.

Painful memories fought for pre-eminence and I took solace from the knowledge that on this occasion we had tickets bearing the right to comfortable seats.

As the journey continued we slowly relaxed, as rekindled memories faded. Elone and Nicolae began to play like children again and I watched them jealously, knowing it was incumbent on me to maintain a distance from such juvenile displays, for they were my personal responsibility now.

It would not do for a guard or other passenger to come by and find three children playing alone. As Izabella had stressed to me, mine was the dutiful role of responsible elder sibling and, if anyone asked, I was to say I was sixteen. When I objected that I barely looked my twelve years, Izabella had shook her head and advised me this was not so, and that I could pass as someone older

I had taken delight in this assurance for, if it is the way of young people to will their years away, my desire for mature years was all the more urgent for that it was driven by need. The need to be able to look after Nicolae and Elone properly, in a way no twelve year old could be expected to manage.

But manage I must, for if previously our only option had been to return to our friends in the forest, even that was now closed as we rumbled cumbersome through the unknown Polish countryside.

We stopped infrequently at stations along the way, few of which I would even venture to pronounce, and I found myself pondering the nature of language. If I had discovered there were words in common betwixt my native Romanian and my newly acquired Polish, still the differences were so many that it was hard to believe we were all but neighbouring countries.

I was deep in contemplation of such imponderables when I felt a tiny hand slip into mine and looked down to see Elone snuggling to my side. A smile played on my lips as I saw Nicolae had fallen asleep on the seat opposite. I crossed over briefly to make him comfortable, wrapping his coat around his shoulders, then returned to where Elone waited patiently.

"I have something for you, Anca," she said as I retook my seat. She thrust a hand into her pocket and extracted a silk purse.

I could not hide my astonishment as she loosened the cord and tipped the contents into the palm of my hand.

"It is from Wojciech. He gave it to me to look after while you were saying goodbye to Izabella."

I took the coins cautiously, hardly daring to believe our good fortune.

As if reading my thoughts, Elone explained, "He said he knew you would not accept any money from him, so he told me to look after it for you. He said that you were too stubborn. Like a mule." She laughed at the simile and I smiled along, knowing he was quite right. Money had been offered, but I had declined most vociferously, intent that we did not draw upon our hosts' meagre resources more than was necessary.

"Elone, you ought not have accepted this," I said, grateful indeed that she had.

"Wojciech said that is what you would say," the child laughed. "That is why he told me not to give it to you until we had been on the train a while. I hope we have travelled far enough, Anca."

I passed my arm around her neck and hugged her tightly. "You did the right thing, Elone. Bless you."

"Are you not going to count the money?"

I looked down at the assortment of coins and shrugged. It was a long time since I had handled money on my own, though I knew that the lei of my native Romania had become all but worthless. I looked at the zloty in my palm and decided for now simply to relish the fact that we had money at all. The amount, its nominal value or its true market worth, was for now unimportant.

I slipped the coins back into the purse and secured it in my coat pocket, drawing Elone to me.

"We can count it later, Elone. Let us rest for now, for we will need all our strength when we get to Krakow. I will need your eager eyes to help find Henryk's home, and I will need your help to look after Nicolae. Will you do that for me?"

She looked up and smiled at me. "Of course, Anca. I will do anything for my friends."

I bent down and kissed her forehead.

"Then shut your eyes and rest, Elone, as I ask. We have a long journey ahead of us."

True to her word Elone did as she was bid, snuggling down and closing her eyes. Very soon she was asleep, leaving me alone with my thoughts to watch the Polish countryside go by.

Dusk became dark but I could not sleep, lost in deep and forbidding thoughts, soothed only by the gentle roll of the carriage as the steaming locomotive drew us on through the still night.

Chapter 44.

The hiss of steam and the screech of locomotive wheels disturbed me and I was at once alert, aware it was daylight once more and we were entering a station.

I wiped the condensation from the window to establish our whereabouts and jumped to my feet as realisation dawned. If hung with Nazi swastikas, still the signs announcing Warsaw's central station were unmistakable.

I shook Elone gently to wake her from her slumber before moving across to perform the same task upon Nicolae.

I knew it was necessary for us to alight at this station and board a second train to complete our journey to Krakow. This much a guard had confirmed to me during the course of the night, when he had come to inspect our tickets.

Fortunately, Izabella and Wojciech had prepared us for just such an eventuality and, with the little ones asleep at my side, I evidently passed for a competent teenager conducting my charges across the countryside. My Polish, if imperfect, aroused no suspicion. The guard was officious and did not try to engage me in conversation beyond the predicted and practiced exchange.

Now, alighting onto the cold platform of Warsaw Central Station, I felt the first hint of fear as the desperate nature of our situation dawned. We were alone, in the capital of a foreign country, surrounded by hurrying Poles and Germans, many of whom wore the hated Gestapo emblem.

I drew Nicolae and Elone to my side and looked about the station for information indicating where we would board the train for Krakow, but nothing was obvious.

Nicolae indicated his need for a toilet and we manoeuvred our way around the station in the hope of finding such a facility. But as we moved from our own train my blood ran cold as I saw a line of cattle trucks on a siding across the way.

The children saw them too and I felt their grips tighten against my palms. Nicolae fell silent, his needs forgotten. Elone tugged at my arm drawing us in the opposite direction and I let her lead the way without objection, searching for comforting words, but none came.

We were half way across the station, fighting our way through the crowd, when loud whistles blew and at once the crowds melted away, people vanishing quickly through exits or moving to the station's borders.

Not realizing what was happening we were slow to respond, and found ourselves suddenly alone in the centre of the station.

Bewildered.

Frightened.

A Polish guard shouted, "You children! Where are your parents?"

In confusion I responded in my native tongue, stopping myself instantly, cursing my carelessness.

Fortunately we were too far distant for the guard to hear, and as he shouted his demand a second time, Elone responded in Polish, "We have lost them in the crowd. One minute they were here with us, now they are gone."

Her quick-witted response saved us from further attention, for the guard gestured angrily for us to clear the concourse, shouting "To one side, now! Do you want to catch the plague from the filthy Jews?"

I grabbed Nicolae's and Elone's hands and bustled them to the side, blending with the waiting crowd before Elone could respond further. "Don't be offended, Elone," I muttered beneath my breath. "He only speaks so because the Nazis are here."

But somehow I knew this ill-feeling to the Jews ran deeper, and I feared that, far from being a help, Elone's command of language and her quick mind might well prove a liability.

As we turned back to watch, long lines of Jews began to file patiently into the station, occupying the concourse with their usual quiet dignity.

I watched with numbed mind as Germans and Poles alike jeered as they filed through, SS guards on either side happy to encourage the abuse, and as the announcement was made for them to chalk their names on their luggage, which would follow them on to Treblinka, memories of Bucharest assailed my mind.

Elone's hand gripped mine tightly. I knew Treblinka was not the place where Mama and we had been bound, but surmised it must be a camp of similar purpose, and looked on with mixed emotions, aware the Jews would be transported in horrific conditions, but jealous too that they would, if they survived the journey, have the chance of a new life on arrival.

I could feel Elone quake, fearful memories etched into her mind, and pushed the children to the back of the crowd, asking in Polish, "Toilet? Where is the toilet, please?"

At first we were ignored, but then someone pointed to a block some metres distant and I guided my charges into its sanctuary, determined they should not be further reminded of the events that marked the last moments we had seen our respective parents alive.

I ushered the children into a feculent cubicle, urging them to make use of the opportunity, for I honestly could not say when another might arise.

Overcome with curiosity I hauled myself onto a ledge and peered through a tiny window affording a view of the station.

As I watched the last Jews crammed into the cattle wagons and the doors closed on them I became alarmed, for now station workers with hand carts began loading the chalk-labelled luggage, only to transport their cargo not on to the waiting train but into a warehouse adjacent to the toilet block we now hid in.

If my Polish was poor, still I was convinced the Jews had been informed, just as we all had back in Bucharest, that their luggage would follow in the final carriage. Yet as the locomotive built up steam and prepared to depart with its cargo of despair, it became obvious to me that the Jews' belongings were not destined to join them.

I could not help but wonder what would these people do when they arrived at Treblinka without their baggage? Without even clothes to change into?

Curiosity compelled me to investigate further. I spoke quietly to Elone, asking her to stay with Nicolae in the toilet block until I returned. I was, I told her, going to find out where we should wait for our train.

I saw the information board proclaiming the time and platform from which our train to Krakow would depart and checking the clock was thankful we had not long to wait.

Perhaps I should have stopped here and returned to my charges, having satisfied my legitimate mission, but the fate of the Jews' luggage strained at my mind, for I owed it to Elone to learn more.

I found myself dallying nonchalantly at the side of the warehouse, looking for a window from where I might gain the insight I needed. There were some splintered wooden pallets, below a high window, down a siding barely visible from the main concourse and I made my way there unnoticed and clambered up to the grime-laden glass, hesitantly peering in.

Though it seemed like seconds, the station clock would confirm I spent nearly fifteen minutes at that window, precariously balanced on the pallets, staring, disbelieving, at the activities revealed.

Chapter 45.

There below me were row upon row of Polish workers emptying the very luggage I had just seen retrieved from the concourse.

Emptying cases and bags, valises and hold-alls, spilling their contents onto rows of tables, where the goods were being sorted, sifted, mixed together regardless of ownership.

If at first the scene seemed one of chaos, luggage being emptied, the contents thrown into baskets and crates, the more I watched the more I saw order in this madness. It became apparent that the belongings were being sifted by value. Jewellery, candelabra and fine pottery were put carefully to one side, under the close supervision of SS guards. Clothes were being sorted, coats and jackets into one basket, shoes to another and so on.

All these personal effects, items I knew just a short while ago had belonged to countless hundreds of Jewish families, were being sorted and separated with callous disregard of their owners' wishes.

Confusion and alarm juggled against one another in my mind as I saw box upon box of photographs, pictures of families, of grandparents, of little children, being tipped into an unmarked crate, piled one load upon another and I knew, somehow I just knew, these mementoes were destined for incineration.

It was a puissant portent of things to come.

In shock I lowered myself to the ground, by now desperately fearful for the children.

Elone grabbed my arm as I rejoined them, unable to hide her concern. "Anca, you are quite pale. What is it? Are you not well?"

I struggled to maintain my composure, forcing the scene from my mind, telling myself I had been mistaken. That the Jews' luggage left on the station concourse and that which I had just seen ransacked were not one and the same.

I clutched Elone to me, and Nicolae too, saying, "Come little ones, I have found the platform we need to wait at. It is just across the way and our train is due very soon." I added, "Remember, children, speak only in Polish while there are people around us. Come, let us make haste."

I led them in silence across the station to the appropriate platform and we waited impatiently for the arrival of our train. The children were quiet, for it was easier to say nothing than employ our limited command of Polish talking among ourselves.

For my part I was too subdued by what I had just witnessed to be inclined to persiflage, so welcomed the young ones' reticence.

At length the locomotive pulled noisily into the station, dragging its ophidian procession in its wake, grinding to a deafening, shuddering halt before us. I was thankful to see it was comprised of passenger carriages, not cattle wagons.

We stood by as passengers alighted then, selecting a sparsely occupied carriage, made ourselves comfortable in a far corner. The information board, though only in Polish and German, had been instructive, and I had established we had not too long a journey ahead. We had by now consumed the provisions Izabella and Wojciech had provided for us and I knew the children would soon feel hungry again.

The other passengers in our carriage were at some distance and, protected by the engine's roar, we were able to converse quietly in our native tongue, though I would not be drawn by Elone's questions as to what had so upset me at the station, rather changing the subject to more pleasant matters.

Elone seemed soon to forget the incident and for my part, if unable to forget, I at least pushed the memory to the back of my mind, enjoying some juvenile word games with the children until at length Nicolae began to yawn and very soon dozed, his head on my lap. I pulled his legs onto the seat to make him comfortable and Elone joined him in this position, engaging in casual chatter until she too succumbed to slumber.

Time passed quickly, or at least stations were tended and soon departed, which was much the same thing for me. I mentally counted off the stations as we stopped each time, having calculated how many preceded Krakow, and knew we would soon be approaching our destination.

I was about to awaken the children in anticipation when a voice boomed out, "Tickets! Passports! Have them ready for inspection!"

I was at once mortified to see a Polish guard advancing along the carriage, accompanied by a Gestapo officer, scrutinizing the travel documents of our fellow passengers.

Panic gripped me, for we were without papers of any sort and I had no confidence I could carry off our deception beyond the most simple of practiced responses.

I looked about me, desperate for inspiration, for some way out of this peril, but realised our only hope was to bluff our way through. The guard on his own I could probably manage, for his attention would be on our tickets, which were in order. Wojciech had seen to that.

But if it were realised we were not Polish nationals then the matter of passports would inevitably be raised and the SS officer would become involved. Bad enough, I knew, to be foreigners in this country, travelling without authorisation. But if Elone's Jewish heritage were realised...

I struck the thought from my mind, for it was unthinkable what might happen. Then, all at once, the guard was at our seat, firing questions too rapidly for me to understand.

I feigned sleepiness, asking him to repeat his query and he did so more slowly for my benefit. As I showed him our tickets he leant across and grabbed at Elone's legs, shoving them from the seat. "Keep your dirty shoes on the floor, child," he shouted angrily, and I quickly leant across and eased Nicolae's feet to the ground, trying not to wake him.

"Ow! You hurt me, you brute!" Elone objected in Polish, indifferent to both the guard's authority and to the presence of the SS officer standing just a few steps away.

Without thinking I urged her to be quiet in my native tongue, my breath held in abeyance as I realised what I had done.

The SS officer was instantly at my side, staring down at us with cold, unfeeling eyes. "That was not Polish, child. Where are you from?"

I knew deception was pointless. "Romania. We are Romanians."

"Name, child?"

"Anca. Anca Pasculata."

He turned on Elone. "And you, little girl? You who think you can talk to your superiors in that way? What is your name?"

My heart all but stopped, praying she would only announce her forename, for to say she was a Pfefferberg would surely seal all our fates.

"Elone," she said.

I interjected quickly, "She is my sister, Elone Pasculata. Please, forgive her rudeness. She is very tired, for we have been travelling some while." I added, "This is my brother Nicolae. Please, Sir, do not disturb him unnecessarily, I beg of you."

The SS officer glared at me. "I will disturb whosoever I wish, child."

He made as if to move towards my brother and Elone immediately placed herself in front of Nicolae, saying, "Leave him alone. He is only six."

The SS man looked surprised by her defiance. He glared at her, as if contemplating his response.

"You are travelling alone?" the guard demanded.

Before I could compose an answer Elone said in Polish, "What are you, stupid? Do you think three children so young would be travelling alone? Our Papa is looking for the toilet." She wagged her finger at the guard as one might chide a small child. "He will be back shortly and I will tell him how you hurt me."

If impressed by her quick mind and command of a foreign tongue I was at the same time mortified by her tone, yet her rudeness proved to work in our favour.

The Gestapo officer leaned forward until he was level with Elone, a hand extracting his whip from its holster. I held my breath.

"Child, you are very loud. Very brash. And so young. You cannot be more than eight, surely."

"I am nine, not eight," Elone declared, meeting his unflinching gaze with fiery eyes.

"Is there no end to your insolence?" the Gestapo officer asked. "I wonder at your father, that he should bring you up so. You would benefit from a good whipping to teach you some manners." He tapped the horse whip unfurled against the palm of his hand. "Perhaps I should give you the benefit of my Aryan upbringing."

"You lay one finger on me and my father will have you thrown off this train," Elone informed him in such confident tone I myself almost believed her. "He is well-connected in both Bucharest and Warsaw, I would have you know, and will have you sent to the eastern front before this day is out."

The officer's mouth fell open, uncertain how to respond. At length he stood back and a smile crept across his cruel mouth. "Consider yourself lucky I am in a good mood today, little girl. You are forthright, and I like you for it. It makes a change to see someone so young stand up for themselves. I tell you, the way these obsequious Jews simper to our every whim is quite sickening at times."

I laid a cautioning hand on Elone's arm, anxious she should not respond to any derogatory comment about her people. She glared at him, but held her tongue.

The SS man demanded, "Your father, which way did he go?"

I was thankful we had not selected an end carriage this time. I gestured behind me, in the opposite direction from where the two men had come.

"That way. He will be back soon. He has our passports with him."

"But you carry your own tickets?" the guard asked. "Is that not a little strange?"

"That was in case you came to us while he was gone," Elone said quickly. "How could he know you would want to see our passports as well?"

The guard seemed satisfied by this explanation, but the SS man peered closely at her.

"Elone, did you say your name was?" He rolled the name around his tongue, savouring it, then, "Elone. Hmmm. It has a certain Semitic ring to it, do you not think?"

My heart missed a beat. I feared we were found out. But once again Elone was to show a maturity and understanding beyond her years.

She stood up angrily, turning on the Gestapo officer and shouted at him at the top of her voice. "Are you calling me a filthy Jew? You ignorant pig!" She jumped onto the seat, shouting down the carriage, "Papa! Papa! This man dares call me a Jew! Papa! Come quickly!"

The guard and SS officer alike reeled in embarrassment, the latter raising his hands to calm her. "That will do, child. I apologise. There is no need to make a fuss. I just wanted to be sure. You know how underhand these Jewish scum can be."

Elone sat down sullenly and I chided her in mock tones of anger. "Elone, behave yourself, or I will tell Papa of your insolence."

The SS man shook his head sadly. "She is spirited, of that there is no doubt."

He turned to me. "Your father, girl. What is his name?"

"Petre," I said. Petre Bogdan Pasculata."

The SS man nodded. "We will have words with him, I think. He should know how ill-mannered his children are in his absence."

"No, please, no," Elone spoke up, evidently enjoying her role play. "He will beat me if you inform him so. I am sorry. Please, I did not mean to be rude."

The SS man smiled, almost sympathetically, though I could not quite bring myself to attribute such a warm emotion to anyone wearing the Gestapo uniform.

He said, "Very well, child, but behave yourself hereon." He brought the whip down hard on his own hand to make the point. "One more word from you and I will see to it you do not sit in comfort the remainder of your journey."

And with this chastisement they turned and walked away.

As they left the carriage I grabbed Elone, hugging her to my breast, unable to hide my delight and amazement at her performance.

"Elone, you were quite wonderful! I cannot believe you spoke Polish so well! And your acting... Where did you learn to conduct yourself so? You should be on a stage! When you threatened to have him sent to the Russian front it was all I could do not to laugh aloud."

Elone basked briefly in my appreciation, but her face quickly became serious again.

"Anca, why do people hate us so? Why is it so wrong to be a Jew?"

I clutched her tightly to me. "I do not know, Elone, honestly I do not know."

Before Elone could ask further imponderables the train began to slow for a station and I calculated we were but one stop from Krakow.

I said, "Elone, I think it would be for the best if we get off here. Krakow is the next stop, but if we wait longer the guard may return. I think it would be tempting fate to try to deceive them a second time."

The station was barely attended, few people disembarking, and we stood by the door waiting until the very last minute before alighting, for fear of being seen by the guard and arousing suspicion.

In this we were to be proven well-judged, for as we dismounted the carriage and the train began to move away I glanced back and saw the guard staring at us before turning to the SS officer and pointing us out.

His incredulous, ruddy face appeared at the window. Anger shone in his eyes and I was mesmerized, watching him run the length of the moving carriage to an unfixed window. I willed the train to hurry, realising our deception had been discovered, fearing the worst.

But as I watched him struggle with the window latch the train gathered speed and was already half way out of the station. The window came down and his angry face appeared through the opening, but by now the locomotive was in full flow, dragging the carriages in its wake and though I could see him shout still his words were inaudible above the scream of the train's whistle and seconds later the whole procession of carriages rounded a bend and were gone.

For perhaps a minute I stood watching, fearing the train would suddenly stop, reverse and bring the Nazi back to us, but as the cloud of steam continued to fade into the distance, colour returned to my cheeks and my pulse began to ease.

Elone too watched, aware how close we had come to being caught, and I clutched her hand tightly, saying, "It is okay, Elone. We are safe now."

Nicolae's hand crept into mine and his voice piped up, "Anca, I'm hungry."

I had all but forgotten my little brother in our moment of crisis, and bent down to pick him up, kissing him on the cheek.

"Oh, little one, I do not know what I should do without you. Of course you are hungry. Come, we will find somewhere to buy food. Then, Nicolae, I am afraid we have a long walk before us."

I put my brother down and gathered both children to my side. "The sooner we get going, little ones, the sooner we will be at Henryk's."

Nicolae asked quietly, "Will Mama be there?"

I desperately wanted to reassure him, but could not bring myself to lie.

"No, little one. We have a little way further to go before we will see Mama again."

Chapter 46.

We selected from a war-ravaged stock of seasonal esculents at a nearby emporium, courtesy of the money Wojciech had bequeathed us, savouring the impromptu picnic.

That night we slept uneventfully in a disused barn, and though it was soon after dawn when we left the farmstead still it was late afternoon when we arrived in Krakow itself. We found Pomorska Street as evening was drawing in, having first located Krakow central railway station, then following the directions Wojciech had left us.

Outside Henryk's house I fussed the children to straighten their clothes and brush the remnants of the hay bed from their hair. We waited patiently for the door to open, Elone at my side, Nicolae coyly hanging behind. The door unlatched and a man stood framed in the entrance, looking down on us with a mixture of surprise and curiosity.

"Henryk? Henryk Brzezinski?"

It seemed only polite to enquire, though I was quite certain it was he, for if many years younger than Wojciech the resemblance was striking.

"And if I am, child? What business is it of yours?"

This was not easy. "I... We... We were sent here by your brother, Wojciech."

Henryk cast his eyes up and down the street warily. "Wojciech? He sent you here? Why would he do that, child?"

"He... That is..." My limited proficiency in his language suddenly deserted me and I lamely proffered the letter in lieu of explanation.

Henryk took the envelope cautiously, studying the hand-writing, then turning his gaze upon us again. "This is from Wojciech?"

"He sends his regards, as does Izabella. I am sorry, but we speak only a little Polish. If you read his letter all will be clear."

Still Henryk stared at us, occasionally diverting his gaze to study the envelope, turning it in his hand as if to determine its content without committing himself to the uncertain fate it would surely reveal.

"You know Izabella too?"

"We stayed as their guests in the forest some six months."

He looked at the envelope a final time then, casting a glance up and down the street, stood aside and ushered us through the door. "Quickly, come in. I confess I do not understand any of this, but it is for the best you are not seen outside, whatever the true nature of your visit."

He led us through to a small room at the back of the house where an aromatic broth simmered gently in a copper marmite upon a small stove.

We savoured the tempting bouquet as we stood there, shuffling awkwardly, uncertain how we should conduct ourselves. Nicolae slipped his hand into mine, still shyly clinging to my side. Elone wandered across to the stove, sniffing longingly at the wholesome broth.

My attention focused on our host, who now ripped the envelope open and extracted the contents. With occasional pauses to study us, as if reading off some description that would confirm our identity, he perused the missive, then, folding it slowly and confining it to the safety of his pocket, he turned to us, a smile for the first time on his lips.

"You must be Anca," he said. "And by default this must be Nicolae, and this Elone. From Romania, no less! Well, well! I cannot pretend to understand what lies behind all this, but if Wojciech believes you are worthy of assistance then, young lady, I am at your service. Are you hungry?"

He glanced at Elone hanging by the stove. "But of course you are. That is plain enough from the way you savour the air. Take off your coats, children, and make yourself comfortable at that table. Let us attend your immediate needs first, after which you can explain precisely how it is you believe I can assist you."

If we had known hunger far worse than that brought on by barely a day without food, still we consumed our broth ravenously, eagerly partaking of second helpings and wiping our bowls clean with a half loaf of salty rye-bread generously supplied.

While we ate Henryk made no enquiry as to the circumstances which brought us to him, intent solely on meeting our pressing needs, occasionally asking after Wojciech and Izabella.

At length he said, "Whatever your purpose here, clearly it is too late to do anything tonight. The young ones are exhausted, Anca. There is a spare bed in the next room which will easily accommodate all three of you. When you have eaten I suggest you put the little ones to sleep, after which you can explain your mission here in your own time."

Elone protested immediately this arrangement, intent on being party to our debate, but within the hour both Nicolae and she were sleeping soundly in the comfort of a large bed.

Once certain they were secure I rejoined Henryk in the adjacent room, accompanied only by a simmering samovar and a dusty gramophone. Henryk prepared us both a tall glass of steaming tea. A scratched record played Strauss quietly in the background, helping to fill the long pauses as we explored one another's acquaintance, but at length the discussion turned to how we had come to be in the forest, heading for Krakow.

Henryk listened with patience and sympathy as I struggled to make sense of events.

As I relived the horror of the train crash and related how the Nazis had fired on the survivors he left his task of rewinding the gramophone and moved across to take my hand, his eyes glistening in the candlelight.

"You poor child. How many in all survived this incident, do you know?"

"Not many, I fear. Nicolae, Elone and myself, obviously, and perhaps a few dozen more..."

"And the girl's parents? Chaim and Golda? You are uncertain if they were even on this train?"

"I cannot know for sure, but Golda was just behind us, with Elone. There were several wagons still to load. I cannot conceive she was not forced aboard with her daughter... And if so..."

I could not bring myself to state the logic of my observation, for I knew I could not face Elone believing her parents had perished. Better to clutch at the faint hope that they were both still alive, however unrealistic that might be.

Henryk asked quietly, "And your own mother, Anca? What of her?"

I struggled to keep my composure. "We were separated from the Jews at Bucharest. It was only Nicolae's brave defence of his friend that found he and I on the same train with them. The Jews were all being forced onto the one train, you understand. Another locomotive waited a short way off. I cannot be sure, but it seemed we would otherwise have been loaded onto the second train, once the first had been filled."

"But you were all bound for the same destination, you say? How can you be so sure?"

I explained how Chaim had first introduced himself to us, on the journey from Medgidia to Bucharest. How he had translated our travel documents while Nicolae and Elone befriended one another.

Henryk leant forward in earnest. "Anca, this is important. Do you remember the name of the camp you were intended for?"

I shook my head. "No, only that it was the same place as Chaim, Golda and dear Elone. That it was in Poland, and that we were first bound for Krakow."

I paused, searching for the words. "Why should they transport people such distances, Henryk? And in such conditions? Why bring Romanians to Poland? It makes no sense to me."

"Do not trouble your pretty head with such matters," Henryk cautioned quickly. "Suffice it to say there are many, many labour camps in this country, my child. Some are as exactly as they claim to be, but others..." He paused, looking into my eyes, then, "Would you like more tea, Anca?"

I declined politely.

"You should, my child. It has brought colour to your cheeks. They are quite incarnadine, though pale just a short while ago."

"These labour camps, Henryk," I persisted. "My mother is at one of them, of this I am convinced. Perhaps, just perhaps, Chaim and Golda too. It is imperative we go there."

Henryk took a deep breath and gripped my hand, struggling with his own words. I wondered what it was he could not bring himself to say.

"Anca," he began hesitantly. "Anca, there are so many camps in these parts, fed by the Krakow rail network. It would be quite impossible to identify which one your mother is in. Quite impossible. I am sorry to take your hope away, but it is a fact."

"But I must know, Henryk. I must find her. If you cannot tell me which camp she might occupy then I shall go to each one myself and ask if she is there."

"It is not that simple, my child. If only it were. Do you know anything at all about these camps, Anca? Have you any idea what is happening here in Poland?"

I shrugged indifferently. What did it matter, so long as Mama, Nicolae and I were reunited? We had lost everything in Medgidia. Could a labour camp in Poland be any worse?

I said, "My mother was a seamstress at one time. A skilled worker. I believe it was a factor in our being sent away. That we, that she, might help the Nazi war effort somehow."

I added quickly, "Please understand, Henryk, it was not something she wanted, especially after what they did to Papa... But without work how could she possibly support Nicolae and I?"

"Anca, there is no need to try justify anything. I too work for the Nazis, though it pains me to admit it. It is not through choice, but of necessity. Our country is under German occupation. Everyone here works for the Nazis. Either that or..."

He paused again. "Or they enjoy the same fate as the Jews."

He looked away, unable to meet my eyes.

"My child, I am a driver by trade. A truck driver. God help me, but I daily deliver and collect goods from these camps. These... These labour camps. Anca, what I am trying to say is..." His words trailed.

"Henryk, please, what is it?"

He shook his head, gulping tea from the tall glass. "I think we have discussed enough for tonight, child. You should rest now."

"But Henryk, you make no sense. What is it you are not telling me?"

He got up slowly, his voice firm. "I have to be up very early, Anca, to begin deliveries. That is my truck you saw across the road. The hour is late and I must rise early. I suggest we continue this conversation tomorrow evening."

I stood up angrily. "No, Henryk, now. Tell me now, what is it that bothers you so? I have a right to know."

He put a hand on my shoulder. "My child, remember your place here, please. You are my guest and you will do as you are asked, for it would be ill-mannered not to. Now you will rest the night, for you surely need it. You can stay here tomorrow and tomorrow night. We will talk again when I return, and discuss how we might resolve your dilemma. After that you must be on your way, for questions will surely be asked if you stay longer."

I opened my mouth to protest but he placed a gentle finger on my lips.

"No dissent, Anca. We will talk again tomorrow evening. Make yourself at home here during the day. I regret my larder is pauce for I was not expecting visitors and I tend to eat on the road, but help yourselves to whatever you may find there. Make sure you all eat well to keep up your strength."

"You are very kind, Henryk."

"Anca, I must insist you remain in the house during the day. There is nothing outside that can be of value to you beyond fresh air, and that is best foregone in the circumstances. It would be most unhelpful, Anca, most unhelpful, if it became common knowledge that three children were here. Awkward questions would be asked and I think you understand well enough that we all could do without that. So please, Anca, please, stay indoors and keep the curtains closed."

"I understand, Henryk. Rest assured we will not venture out without your permission."

"Should you by chance be discovered here, if by an unexpected caller perhaps, then say simply that you are my nephew and nieces, kin of my brother Wojciech and his wife Izabella. Of course they are far too old to have children your age, but no-one else will know that fact."

I nodded my complicity.

"Finally, Anca, I'm sure you do not need to be told, but I cannot stress this strongly enough. On no account let it be known, even if you need lie to preserve the fact, that Elone is a Jew. Not here. Not in Krakow."

I could not quite fathom the importance of this command, for while I knew Jews were held in low esteem by the Nazis the emphasis Henryk placed on Elone's persuasion remaining secret seemed unduly severe. Obviously we would not wish the SS to be aware of her heritage, but was it so important to anyone else?

I made plain my query and Henryk took my hand with both of his, clasping my wrist.

"Anca, please try to understand. There are no Jews left in Krakow."

Chapter 47.

The roar of Henryk's truck outside the window announced dawn's arrival.

As the rhythm of the throbbing engine faded into the distance I knew we had the house to ourselves. I washed and prepared a light breakfast for the three of us, laying the table before calling the little ones to order.

Nicolae was much refreshed from his long sleep and consumed his meal with relish, but Elone picked over her breakfast disinterestedly.

I asked, "Elone, are you not well? Have you lost your appetite?"

Without looking up, she said, "What did Henryk mean, Anca? Why are there no Jews left in Krakow?"

My own appetite was gone in an instant and I went to her side. "Elone, I had no idea you heard us. I am so very sorry."

"I did not mean to listen, only I could not sleep, the walls are thin and the night still. But I do not understand, Anca. How can there be no Jews left? This is such a big city. What did he mean?"

I was unable to offer explanation, only solace. By now I had my suspicions, but they were nascent ideas not yet fleshed out by tangible fact and I would not, I was determined, frighten the child with my inchoate understanding of events.

I said simply, "We cannot know for sure, Elone, we cannot know. But perhaps he meant they have all been transferred to the many labour camps he spoke of." That much seemed certain, but I added less confidently, "For their own good. To give them hope, work, until the war is over."

"Elone, why are you crying?" The question was asked by Nicolae, who had the advantage over me in facing the girl, whereas I now stood just behind her, my arms draped around her shoulders.

I leant round and wiped her tears away with a napkin. "Do not cry, dear Elone." I added in a whisper inaudible to my brother, "Please, Elone, do not cry in front of Nicolae, for he looks up to you so."

At this Elone stifled her tears and put on a brave smile, but she could not help but tender a final question. Wrapping her fingers gently around mine she asked quietly, "Anca, will I ever see my Mama and Papa again?"

What possible answer could I give? There was only one.

"I do not know, Elone. I honestly do not know."

I felt her fingers tightly clutch mine and I prepared myself for her distress, but once again the child foiled my expectations. Releasing my hand, she turned to my brother saying, "Let's play in the back room, Nicolae, while Anca tidies the kitchen, otherwise we will only be in the way."

They left together, Nicolae boisterous, Elone proving her thespian inclinations once more and joining with his gleeful cries, but as she turned in the doorway to briefly glance at me her tear-filled eyes told a different story.

As the door closed behind them I said quietly, "You will never be in the way, Elone. Neither of you will ever be in the way."

Chapter 48.

Nicolae's laughter proved infectious and very soon the sombre mood of the house had been replaced by a more cheerful atmosphere. But after a few hours we had exhausted our entertainments and longed to be outside.

Though we kept the curtains closed as Henryk had asked we could not help but note the sun was beaming down on a pleasant autumn day, the clouds all but banished from the sky, and we longed to play beneath it. I fended Nicolae's demands to go into the street as best I could. Inevitably, boredom was quick to manifest itself, and I suggested we play at tidying the house, a proposition well-received by the children.

In fact Henryk exhibited a most respectable domesticity, but it could hardly cause harm to unleash Nicolae and Elone with a besom and feather duster, and would at least keep them occupied until our host returned.

In this I was to prove well judged, for the activity engaged the young ones for much of the afternoon and I too joined in, relishing mundane domestic chores I would once studiously have avoided.

It was whilst engaged in one such task, polishing an oak cabinet that had known finer days, that I made my discovery.

Quite by accident I knocked a sheaf of papers onto the floor, scattering them across the boards such that it was necessary to pick them up one by one. Of course I had no intent or interest in perusing them, and merely undertook to put them back as I had found them.

Thus scanning the sheets for some indication of order I became aware I was holding Henryk's delivery schedules. If my capacity to read Polish was even less developed than my verbal skills, still I quickly realised this was a list of Nazi labour camps, not just in Poland but across Europe, some of which were marked with Henryk's name.

From somewhere deep in my mind came the thought that the camp Mama had been sent to might be listed here. While I could not remember its name I knew Mama had told me, once, the day before our departure from Medgidia. I had taken no notice at the time, for it meant nothing to me then. But now... My first, hurried scans of the lists of names produced no result and I tried again more slowly, sounding out each name in the hope of recognition.

The list seemed endless and as I read them out the sheer scale of the Nazi operations began to sink in, for it covered countries from Poland to Austria and included even Germany itself. Treblinka; Gross-Rosen; Sobibor; Belzec; Dachau; Pirszkow; Bergen Belsen; Mauthause; Buchenwald; Majdanek; Chelmno and on and on.

These names meant nothing to me, however, and I was beginning to lose hope when suddenly it was there in front of me. Suddenly, unquestioningly, this one name stood out from the others and I knew this was the camp Mama had been bound for. If my heart leapt at this realization, how much more my pulse raced when I realised Henryk was a designated driver for this route!

I rushed out of the room yelling to Elone and Nicolae, determined they should share my discovery, but halted myself as I reached the door, remembering that, even if Mama was there, in all likelihood Chaim and Golda had perished on the train. I could not raise Elone's hopes.

"What is it Anca? What is it?" Elone and Nicolae came racing to attend my excited tones.

"It is nothing, children. I am sorry. I thought I had found something of interest, but I was mistaken. Go back to your play."

"We are not playing, Anca," Nicolae said indignantly. "We are working hard! Do you think Henryk will be pleased when he gets back? When he sees how hard we have worked?"

I smiled reassuringly. "I am sure he will, little one."

Elone eyed me with suspicion, clearly not taken in by my change of tone, but she kept her thoughts to herself. Not for the first time I found myself wondering just how deep ran this child's understanding.

Chapter 49.

By when Henryk arrived home I could hardly contain my excitement, but in deference to Elone I kept quiet about my discovery and made polite conversation.

Nicolae and Elone proudly showed Henryk their work and he beamed broadly as he examined the fruits of their labour, adding kind words. Of course I could not expect, nor did I want, the children to be rewarded for their endeavours, but was delighted nonetheless when Henryk slipped his hand into his pockets and flipped a coin to each child as a token of his appreciation. He turned to me but I put up a restraining hand, assuring him his kindness in receiving us was reward enough.

I helped him prepare tea, advising we would not want too much, for I had no wish to deplete his larder further, and we settled to a light collation, over which he questioned the three of us about life in Romania, patient with Nicolae's poor Polish; admiring Elone's competence; studiously avoiding the subject of family.

After our meal Henryk wound the gramophone and Elone and Nicolae danced, after a fashion, to Hungarian waltzes while Henryk and I partook of hot tea from the samovar. A gramophone was a luxury I had only dreamt of in Medgidia and Nicolae, who had never seen such a thing before, was fascinated by this box that emitted music, delighting in winding it up after each play.

Both children became excited and loud, but my move to hush them prompted a restraining hand from Henryk. I realised his aim was to fatigue the children that they would soon be asleep, the better for us to talk of more serious matters and so I encouraged the children to dance even more energetically, until at last, as darkness drew in, they retired from the floor exhausted and my proposal of bed was eagerly received.

Within the hour both the little ones were fast asleep and, this time first ensuring Elone was indeed slumbering, I crept back to join Henryk once more. He turned the music low, poured another glass of steaming tea each and we settled down to our concerns.

I could hardly contain my excitement and began with a confession to clear my conscience and bring matters immediately to a head.

"Henryk, there is something I must tell you. Please do not think I was deliberately prying, but I happened upon your schedule of deliveries this day and looked through them."

He dismissed my admission with a wave of his hand. "They are of no consequence. Just my work schedules. They are in no way private or personal, Anca. There is no need for concern."

I felt obliged to explain anyway. "I was dusting the cabinet when I knocked them to the floor. I picked them up, trying to sort them back into order and that was when I realised what I was holding." I could contain myself no longer. "Henryk, I know which camp my mother is at now. I recognized the name as soon as I saw it on your list. She is in Auschwitz-Birkenau."

Chapter 50.

Henryk's face paled visibly. His glass trembled in his hand and for fully a minute he stared at me, seemingly unable to speak.

"Henryk, what is it? What is wrong?"

At last he said, "Anca, are you sure about this. How can you be so certain?"

"Mama told me, on the day we received the news. I had completely forgotten the name, for it meant nothing to me at the time. I saw it written on the papers Chaim read to us on the train from Medgidia, also. So when I saw it written on your schedule I recognized it immediately." I added excitedly, "Henryk, it is on your list. I saw your name by it. You are due there tomorrow. You must take us when you go."

Henryk stood up, pacing the floor, unwilling to look at me. "You are certain of this, Anca? That it was Auschwitz? You are not mistaken?"

"Quite certain. Mama, all of us, were bound for Auschwitz-Birkenau. I remember it clearly now, having seen the name again."

I could not sit still, but jumped up and grabbed Henryk's arm. "Do you not see? If Mama was not on the first train, the train that crashed, but on the second, as I believe she must have been, then she will surely be there now, working as a seamstress, wondering if she will ever see her children again."

Henryk stared into the distance, his face void of expression.

I added, "And maybe, just maybe, Elone's parents also arrived there. Henryk, we must go there tomorrow. Please say you will take us with you."

At this request Henryk took me by both arms and held me steady, for the first time looking directly at me. I saw tears in his eyes and my excitement gave way to apprehension.

"Anca... I do not know how to say this, so help me God, I do not."

He stared at me, unable to collect his thoughts into words. Finally, "Anca, I have been inside these camps. I take deliveries to them and collect the goods they produce for distribution." He paused, as if this ought to be sufficient explanation.

I looked into his eyes, not understanding. "So?"

Henryk chose his words slowly. "There are different types of camps, Anca. Some, like Plaszow, are simply labour camps, geared to war production. Others are... They are..."

"Henryk, what is it? Tell me what they are."

"I am sorry, Anca, I cannot. It would be wrong of me to take away your hope."

I grabbed his hands, imploring his attention. "Henryk, you make no sense. What is it? You must tell me."

"No, Anca. That is enough. I will not discuss the matter further. Tomorrow I will make arrangements for you all to return to stay with Wojciech and Izabella. You will remain with them until the war is over and then, perhaps, God willing, you will all be reunited with your families again."

"No, Henryk! No! You will take us to Auschwitz when you go. Drop us at the gate if need be and we will make our own enquiries from there. We are not the helpless children you seem to think, for we have come this far on our own. All I ask is that you take us to the gate. That much you must do for us. Please, I implore you."

Henryk shook his head, again unwilling to meet my gaze. "It is quite out of the question. Auschwitz-Birkenau is no place for children. No place at all." He took my arm. "Anca, if your mother has a skill as you say, if she is a good seamstress, then perhaps she is indeed there today. But children are not tolerated at Auschwitz and I will not in any circumstance take you there. Were it Plaszow I might consider your request, but not... Not to Auschwitz."

I screamed at him, unable to control my emotions. "Why are you doing this, Henryk? You who have been so good to us? Why would you deny us now?"

The gramophone needle ground to a halt but no-one was concerned to tend it. Henryk looked into the distance, as if contemplating a range of responses. At last he said, "Typhus is rampant at Auschwitz, Anca. It is responsible for many deaths there."

Through streaming tears I implored his conscience. "Henryk, would you have our parents die of this disease not even knowing their children are alive and well?"

"I am sorry, but I will not be responsible for taking you to your..." He stopped, unwilling to finish the sentence, shaking his head in sorrow. "No, child, no. I will not even consider it. You will do as you are told, Anca. There is a war raging, lest you had not noticed. There is good reason to suppose it will soon be over, for the Russians are advancing on the Polish border, but until that time you will stay with my brother. He and Izabella will care for the three of you until this nightmare is over. I will pay him myself for your board, so you need not object on those grounds. No arguments, Anca. The matter is not open to negotiation."

I screamed hysterically, "But our Mama! We are so close! We have not come all this way only to be turned back at the last minute! No, Henryk! No! You will take us there! You must. You will drive us to —"

The palm of his hand caught me across the side of the face and stopped my scream instantly. It was not meant as punishment, rather a means to halt my hysteria, but I ran from the room sobbing and flung myself onto the bed between Elone and Nicolae, uncaring if I woke them or not.

I could not understand why Henryk, who until now had shown us such kindness, was now so ill-disposed to our intentions. Confused, sobbing, I placed an arm around the sleeping children and hugged them to me.

Chapter 51.

It was dark and the city stood quiet. Somehow a plan had already formed in my mind. I slipped quietly from the bed, lighting a candle to illuminate my path, past Henryk's room from where I could hear him lightly snore, to where I had that previous afternoon stumbled across the delivery schedules.

I paused only to listen should anyone stir, then rifled through the papers until I found the sheets I wanted to study. By the candle's scant light I struggled to make sense of the detail. It was clear enough Henryk was bound for Auschwitz-Birkenau that very morning, as I had initially supposed. Further study revealed he would first go to Plaszow to collect a consignment of enamelware before going on to Auschwitz itself, there to deliver these goods and return with a cargo of clothing. My heart leapt at this news, for it was possible the very clothing he would collect might be in part Mama's handiwork.

Any residual doubt or hesitation was dispelled at this prospect. It was the light of hope that flickers eternal, driving me on now to pursue my bold plan.

I selected a blank sheet of paper and procured a pen, then sat down and wrote a brief note of gratitude to Henryk, thanking him for his kindness, but explaining that, if he would not take us to Auschwitz himself then we had no choice but to make our own way there. Thanking him a final time I promised to return to see him when the war was over, if at all possible. I signed my name, folded the sheet and placed it carefully on the table where he could not miss it in the morning.

Creeping back to the bedroom I roused Nicolae and Elone, urging them to be silent and, ensuring they were warmly dressed, escorted them through the house and out of the door into the dark night.

Only once outside could I offer any explanation. I said simply, "Nicolae, I think I know where Mama is, though I urge you not to raise your hopes, for I could be wrong."

Nicolae's eyes lit up. "Really, Anca? Will we see her soon? Please tell me we will."

"I cannot promise, Nicolae, but I hope so. I very much hope so."

Elone looked up at me, eyes imploring. "Anca?"

I brought her to my breast and hugged her. "It would be wrong of me to encourage false hope, Elone. It may be we will find your parents too, but I cannot with honesty say we will." I added, as if to offer consolation, "Henryk believes the war will soon be over, Elone. Then, perhaps, we will know for sure. Until then, my friend, my dear friend, you have Nicolae and I, and we you."

"I understand, Anca," Elone said quietly, fighting back the tears.

We huddled by the side of the house while I scanned the road, quickly sighting Henryk's truck. As I had hoped, the wagon was of an open construction with a canvas cover and I pointed out the vehicle to my charges, adumbrating my plan.

"Henryk is to drive to a camp later today to deliver and collect goods. I believe we will find Mama there. He will not have us ride with him so we have no alternative but to become stowaways on his truck and let him deliver us unawares."

Nicolae was open-mouthed at this news. "We are going to ride in that big truck? That big truck right there, Anca? That one there!"

"Hush, little one, hush," I chided. "Do you remember how we played in the forest, before that nasty wolf came upon us? How we pretended to be invisible, so no-one would know we were there? Well we are to play that game again. But this time we will be hiding in the back of Henryk's truck!"

"Without him knowing it, Nicolae! In secret!" Elone added excitedly and at first I thought she too had fallen for my story, but her eyes revealed her true thoughts and I realised once again she was play-acting, for my little brother's benefit.

Chapter 52.

Many hours were spent shivering beneath the tarpaulin before the angry slamming of the cabin door alerted us to the new dawn. As Henryk climbed into his seat and made himself comfortable at the wheel, just the other side of the thin panel that separated cabin and wagon we could hear his loudly voiced imprecations, indifferent to our presence, clearly angered by our impromptu departure.

"That stupid girl! That stupid, stupid girl! She will have them all killed before the week is out! Why did I not tell her? Spell out the truth to her? That even if she by some miracle finds her own mother, the Jew's parents are long since dead. To tell her that no Jew leaves Auschwitz alive."

His words were lost as the engine fired into life and coughed its dirty fumes into the quiet dawn. Above the roar of the engine we could not even hear ourselves speak, let alone what else Henryk might be blaming himself for, but what we had already heard was mind-numbing.

I could barely believe my ears, hoping, praying, I had misheard, or if I had not that at least Elone had been too sleepy to make sense of his remarks.

But as I turned from Nicolae to my young friend Elone I realised she was sobbing, and had heard every word.

Talk was pointless, even had she been able to hear me above the roar of the truck's engine, for no words could offer adequate comfort at such a time. I brought her head to my shoulder and we cried together until we could cry no more.

Chapter 53.

There was no way of telling time as the vehicle negotiated the pitted roads out of Krakow, though from a gap between the tarpaulin sheets I could snatch glimpses of the outside world. Conversation was not possible, for the only occasions we might hear one another, when the truck stopped, we knew we could be heard by our driver with equal ease.

Henryk's stark comments, intended for no-one's ears but his own, would not fade from my mind and I knew Elone too shared my thoughts. Nicolae was thankfully indifferent to our plight, rather enjoying the subterfuge of the journey and obtaining some boyhood delight from the uncomfortable ride, so I was at least able to lend my undivided attention to my friend.

We held hands, touch communicating emotions words could never do justice to, and we drew strength from one another's presence.

I knew, very soon, we would have to make a decision, whether to go on with our bold but increasingly reckless plan, or to surrender ourselves to Henryk's responsibility at this late stage, with the inevitable return to the care of Wojciech and Izabella.

If everything had seemed so simple just hours before, suddenly it was so very complex. The true nature of Henryk's prevarication the previous evening was now apparent, and while I still believed that Nicolae and I would find Mama upon arrival at Auschwitz, Elone's hopes had been cruelly rent asunder.

Images of the depredation of the Jews' luggage at Warsaw station were slowly beginning to make sense to me, and if the whole picture was as yet unclear it was still plain enough that, for the Jews at least, Auschwitz was intended to be their final resting place. I imagined they would be made to work until, quite literally, they dropped, for such cruel brutality by the Nazis was no longer beyond my ability to conceive.

But now I was faced with the dilemma of determining Elone's fate, and with hers ours. It would be quite impossible for us to present ourselves to Henryk and hope he would take Elone back with him but allow Nicolae and I to continue on to Auschwitz-Birkenau.

Yet the alternatives were stark: either we all return to the forest home of Wojciech and Izabella and remain there until the war's final days, or all three of us continue the journey to Auschwitz.

Much as I wanted her to come, much as I wanted, needed, her company, so too I knew that at best she would face only heartbreak when we arrived at our destination. And at worst...

Henryk's words would not leave my thoughts.

"No Jew leaves Auschwitz alive."

Chapter 54.

It was not a decision I could make on her behalf and I resolved to raise this with Elone at the first opportunity, for Henryk would surely need to stop and leave the truck soon, for fuel, food or to meet nature's call.

But when we next stopped I peered cautiously through the tarpaulin to be greeted by the legend *Zwangsarbeitslager Plaszow*. Then, without warning, we were driving through the heavily-guarded gates of the Nazi labour camp.

Suddenly we were tense, the Rubicon crossed. To be discovered now would surely mean ours and Henryk's detention by the SS and if I could hardly bear contemplate the possible consequences for Nicolae and I, the fate Elone faced was quite unthinkable.

I grabbed both children and brought them alongside me, a hand over each mouth, unwilling to trust either child in these dire circumstances. In doing so I drove home to them the importance of their total silence, and they made no protest.

From our hiding place we heard the canvas cover of the wagon pulled back and men shouting orders, some in German, some in Polish. At any moment I expected our huddled bodies to be exposed to the merciless gaze of the SS, and I could not drive from my mind memories of the Nazis spraying the dead and injured with bullets after the train crash those many months before. My whole body trembled and I could feel the children tremor likewise.

Suddenly the wagon floor rocked and I realised laden pallets were being loaded onto the rear of the wagon, pushed back towards us. I held my breath, realising we were about to be crushed by the cargo. As the tarpaulin over us began to push up against our bodies I began to silently pray.

If I had seen too much evil already to believe my prayers should suddenly be answered now, still it was surely a miracle that, even as we were forced against the cabin wall and I was about to cry out and declare our presence, the pallets' advance stopped and we heard the canvas drag back across the wagon's roll bars.

As the engine started up we breathed again, struggling from under the tarpaulin into the semi-darkness of the wagon. Just how close we had come to death or discovery was now apparent, for there was hardly room for us to sit up, so little space was left between us and the cabin wall.

Again too noisy to talk we huddled together, three frightened children, desperate for guidance, but in the sure knowledge our options were few. We drove only a short way across the camp before the vehicle stopped again. The engine switched off and I heard Henryk climb from his cabin and call out for someone to sign his documents. From the gap in the tarpaulin I could just see him, some way distant, in conversation with a guard, and knew this was my only opportunity to consult my companion.

"Elone, dear friend, our fate rests with you now. I will surrender us all to Henryk's tender mercy once we clear this camp, if that is your wish, that you may return to Izabella and Wojciech. They will care for you, Elone. They will look after you as if you were their own, I promise you."

She took my hand. "And if I did, Anca? What of you? What would you do?"

I answered without hesitation. "I would somehow make my way to Auschwitz still, with Nicolae. I have to, Elone, please try to understand. For all that we now know, still it is there, I am certain, Nicolae and I will learn the fate of our own mother."

Her fingers clasped tightly around mine. "Izabella and Wojciech are kind people, Anca, but they are not my family, nor could they ever be so."

She peered at me through the dim light and I could see her eyes glisten. "You are my family now, Anca. You and Nicolae. You are all I have. All I need. I will go with you, wherever you must go." She leant across and kissed first me, then Nicolae, on the forehead, saying, "My sister. My brother."

Chapter 55.

Cramped by the pallets we had no choice but to sit upright for the duration of the journey and I found myself drawn to the gap in the tarpaulin which afforded a view of the passing countryside.

We had travelled only a few minutes beyond Plaszow before encountering a steep hill and were slowed to a walking pace, the engine straining to haul its heavy cargo against the unforgiving slope. Peering out, indifferent to the dull scenery, I realised we were passing lines of Jews, easily identified by their clothes, being marched at gunpoint along the road.

Our speed was such that I could study each one individually and I found myself doing just that, willing one of them to be Chaim or Golda, hope winning a futile battle against reason in my mind.

Of course I recognized no-one and as the anonymous faces continued to pass us despair won out. But as we reached the brow of the hill and began to gather speed once more I was suddenly staring in horror at the scene unfolding just a short distance away.

I looked back the way we had come, unable to believe my senses. Yet there could be no doubt at what I was witnessing. There before me, distant enough not to make out every detail but still close enough to allow no room for mistake, the Jews, as they arrived at a given spot in a field across from the road, were being made to strip at gunpoint and, when completely naked, men, women and children alike, were lined up in neat rows and then mercilessly gunned down with machine-gun fire.

As the truck eased on to a level ground and the strain of the engine relaxed we could hear the guns fire in short bursts and I found myself placing my body across the side of the truck for fear Elone or Nicolae would want to see the cause of the commotion.

I watched helplessly, in morbid fascination, as Jews fell, their naked bodies exploding in a frenzy of blood as bullets ripped them open, to be placidly replaced by their fellows, while behind them others stripped and still more filed into view to take their place. Even as they did so bulldozers pushed the fallen bodies unceremoniously into a pit.

I could not decide which was the more incomprehensible: the slaughter taking place as I watched, adjacent to a public road as if a commonplace act; or the way the Jews continued to march with quiet dignity to their inevitable deaths.

Seconds later the view was obscured by rows of birch trees and very soon we were long past that dreadful place, the images consigned to memory, from where they would not easily depart. As we trundled on through the Polish countryside I could not strike the scene from my mind, and tried to find reason, some logic, some semblance of sanity that might make sense of what I had just seen.

But such a task was impossible, for in truth there was none.

Chapter 56.

ARBEIT MACHT FREI.
I knew no German, but would later learn these words, wrought in iron above the entrance, stated optimistically 'work sets you free'. These black gates, the pallid grey soil and a nauseating smell the like of which I had never encountered before, were my first impressions of Auschwitz-Birkenau as we reached our final destination.

The truck pulled up a little beyond the main gate and amidst loud exchanges in Polish and German I managed to establish that Henryk was being taken to the administrative quarters. In the silence that ensued I guessed we were alone. There was not a moment to lose, for Henryk and the guard might return at any time, and we edged our way hesitantly around the pallets to the rear of the truck.

I dropped myself to the floor and reaching up plucked first Nicolae then Elone from the tail board and as one we slipped beneath the truck's undercarriage, there to study our terrain and judge our next move. The children, sensing the parlous nature of our circumstance, performed magnificently, murmuring not a word, each child responsive to my every unstated gesture.

There was a hut a short way distant, raised from the ground to protect against damp and we raced for it across grey mud rutted by heavy vehicles. Stooping low for fear of attracting attention, we dived as one beneath its shadow.

As our heart beats slowed and we found our breath again, the noisome empyreuma that hung over us violently assaulted our nostrils. It clung to our clothes, permeating every nook and cranny of the complex, leaving no escape from its presence.

At first we, all of us, heaved at its contractions and, though we soon became accustomed to its presence at Auschwitz, it was a uniquely cloying, putrescent stench that would find an indelible imprint in our memories.

Nor was it the only bizarre feature about this place, for though the sky was blue in the distance the air around us, even beneath the hut under which we sheltered, was filled with a mixture of ash, cinder and ecru flakes which I quickly realised were responsible for the strange colour of the soil.

Nicolae whispered, "Anca, I am hungry," and I was reminded, for it was so easy to forget, that he was a child of just six years, void of even the limited understanding Elone and I enjoyed.

Elone said quietly, "It will be some time before Anca can get us anything to eat, Nicolae, so please be patient. Try to rest now, to sleep, then when darkness falls we can search for food."

"And for Mama too, right, Anca? And for Mama too?"

I leant across and kissed his forehead. "We will try, little one, I promise you we will try."

He seemed reassured by this show of confidence, for he stretched out beside me on the hard ground and, slipping his hand into Elone's, closed his eyes, sleep quickly consuming his fatigued body. How I envied this ability to succumb to sleep almost at will, for it was by far the best way to ease the pain. I smiled at Elone and she smiled back.

When she was sure Nicolae was quite asleep she whispered, "Anca, do you really believe you will find your mother here?"

It was a question I would have preferred to avoid. Thus proffered I had no choice but to consider a response.

I rolled across and lay against her, wrapping one arm around her shoulder, my other hand gently stroking Nicolae's hair. Somehow, here in the very heart of Auschwitz, hiding like fugitives beneath a wooden hut on pain of death were we to be discovered, I felt secure and confident.

Looking deep into Elone's eyes I said, "We can only hope, Elone, for the future is unknowable. But consider this. If you are now my sister and I yours, then Mama is mother to all three of us. If we should find her then, I promise you Elone, she will be your mother too."

Elone clutched my hand tightly. "Elone Pasuclata," she said and smiled. "Yes, I like that. I like that very much."

I reached to my collar and retrieved the necklace and amulet Raisa had presented me, placing it over Elone's head.

"This was given me by my best friend, Raisa, that I might remember her by it. I would like you to wear it for me, Elone, as my new sister."

Elone took the amulet in her tiny hand. "I will treasure it, Anca, until the day you and Raisa meet again, when I shall return it to her for you."

And so saying she rolled tight against me, and we lay quiet an untold time.

Chapter 57.

We were soon benighted, dusk prematurely advanced by
the strange cloud of fumes that hung over the camp. The
generators roared and the spotlights of the guard towers
dissected the complex into incandescent ranges delineated by
sharp, deep shadows.

I knew our time had come.

I mustered the children and, stressing the need for absolute
silence and supreme caution, led them to the very edge of our
shelter, where we stopped, hesitant, the younger ones
awaiting my instruction.

I had no concept of direction, no plan beyond finding a
hiding place more secure, and acted accordingly. We crept
into the dark shadows and edged our way, hardly daring to
breathe, to the end of the hut, there to purchase a better view
of the camp's layout.

It was obvious enough we should move away from the
perimeter gates, but barbed wire fences loomed in all
directions, intermittently patrolled by armed guards. The
perimeter fences were still more securely policed, with fierce
dogs as well as soldiers, while searchlights swept the outer
boundary incessantly.

The inner compounds were clearly less well guarded and I
knew it was in this direction we should head. Though I could
see no evidence of a passage through the fences I knew there
must be one and cautiously led the children as far as I dared,
fearing at any minute a heavy hand on my shoulder or even,
though I struggled hard to keep the thought at bay, a bullet in
my back.

But we were to prove blessed, for neither event transpired and, over the course of several hours, we managed to steal our way further into the camp, running from shadow to shadow, stopping each time to regain our breath and restore our composure.

Our task was made all the easier for that the camp's workers were kept in barracks at night, and the few guards we did encounter were more concerned with their own private preoccupations than searching the shadows for intruders. All security was geared to the opposite purpose, to prevent anyone leaving. An observation that left me quietly uneasy, reinforcing my belief that, whatever danger we might face, there could be no turning back.

Just how far we had smuggled ourselves onto the site, or what function the buildings against which we hid might have I could only guess, but already it was becoming clear Auschwitz-Birkenau was a complex of immense proportions, stretching on and on whichever way one looked, though still the true scale of the camp, like the enormity of its purpose, had yet to be realised.

Many of the buildings were raised constructions, affording useful hiding places for us, and occasionally, as we hid beneath one, we could hear German voices, laughing and joking as they partook their evening repast. The smell of hot food managed to penetrate our nostrils even over the fetid, heavy atmosphere that hung all around us, screening the sky, obscuring a bicephalous moon.

Inevitably Nicolae was reminded of his hunger and I was thankful once again for Elone's ability to occupy my little brother's attention.

From our hiding place beneath one such hut I became aware of a strange glow on the horizon, which I concluded must be a furnace, perhaps of an iron foundry or like industry.

While hardly anticipating Mama would be employed in such an operation this was the first suggestion of where the camp's workers might be found, and that it appeared to be operating through the night was all the more encouraging, raising the hope we might be able to approach someone under cover of darkness and at least establish the location of the women's quarters.

This empyreal glow thus became our goal and we began a slow, tortuous progress towards it. As ever the children were stoic, Elone indomitable of spirit, comforting Nicolae when his determination flagged.

Several times we came close to discovery, for many were the occasions when we had to race across open areas where no shadows reached, and even to smuggle ourselves through guarded gates as we crossed from one compound to the next. Fortunately the guards seemed more concerned with huddling together to share a cigarette than to perform their duties, secure in the presumption that no-one, least of all three children, would even then be making their way across the camp.

As we continued the glowing sky loomed ever closer until we could at last see the chimneys from which the candescence emerged, and with it the fetid fumes and filth-laden, ashen smog that descended everywhere, coating everything, permeating our clothes to our very skin.

So obsessed had we been in pursuit of the furnaces that time had passed unnoticed. But as dawn began to break we slipped beneath the floor of a raised hut for a final time that night. In hushed whispers I advised the children it would be necessary to remain here through the day, until night fell once more.

Elone received this news bravely, but for Nicolae the strain was too much and he began to sob, no longer able to contain his emotions, no longer able to constrain his physical needs. He, we all, were tired, hungry and spiritually drained and I knew that lassitude would be our undoing, if I could not soon make good our plight. For now, however, all I could do was offer quiet comfort.

As I turned to do so I found Elone once more had assumed this role and it sunk home to me now that this young girl, though no relative by blood, was far the better parent to my little brother, for he clung to her now as he had once, but no longer, clung to me, and it became clear he treasured her comforts more than mine.

For an instant I felt jealousy impinge sharp on my heart, but I banished the emotion with some effort, knowing I could not fulfil the role of mother to Nicolae and at the same time lead us all to ultimate salvation.

I gathered the two children to me, kissing them both, and said without conviction, "We will be fine, little ones, I promise you."

Chapter 58.

The dawn's rays were still struggling to banish the dark night when the reveille sounded. I heard stirrings in the cabin above our heads and in the distance saw soldiers approach this and adjacent barracks, unlocking doors and shouting commands in harsh German. In minutes the concourse was a hive of chaotic activity as labourers, all men, crossed back and forth to the latrines.

If relieved to find we were at last in the workers quarters, my fears were confirmed that the camp was segregated, for there were no women or children to be seen, and I became concerned once more for our security.

I had hoped somehow to mingle the three of us with the internees of the camp to allow us freedom of movement that we might try trace Mama. The all-adult, all-male presence clearly necessitated a reappraisal of this plan.

But before I could reconsider our options whistles shrieked and suddenly men were running to the centre of the concourse and assuming pre-determined lines, tardiness rewarded by the butt of a soldier's rifle or by the whip of men bearing the word Kapo on their sleeves.

As we watched the men line up like school children at assembly, to be head-counted and lectured on the day's duties, I could see they all bore sign of ill health and malnourishment, some quite skeletal. Even as I watched, as if to confirm my worst fears, a worker in an outside line began to waver and fell to the ground, his breathing laboured, his body weak.

At once two or three men around him rushed to his aid but were driven off by two Kapos, hitting out at these Samaritans with their hand whips, pushing them away from the fallen worker. Then, in scenes painfully reminiscent of Elone's treatment at Bucharest station, a Kapo began to kick the fallen man, screaming and shouting at him in a language I knew to be neither Polish nor German.

A single gunshot cracked across the camp, bringing everything to a halt. The two Kapos stood upright as a Nazi officer approached. The workers as one turned forward and stood to attention, all eyes front, now not daring even to cast a sympathetic glance to their fallen colleague.

I clutched Nicolae and Elone to me, burying their heads against my chest, determined they should not witness the scene I now anticipated, but I could not tear my own eyes away. If I knew how this scene would end, still I watched in morbid fascination, trying to follow the shouted exchange between the Kapos and the German officer who now brusquely addressed them.

They both pointed accusingly at the man on the ground. Without further debate the officer produced his pistol, fired a single shot to the back of the fallen worker's head, turned and walked away. Even before the blood had finished pumping one of the Kapos had seconded two men from the assembled ranks to drag the body away.

Suddenly a further whistle blew and the ordered assembly became chaos again, men running to their barracks, to emerge seconds later carrying enamel mugs and bowls and I realised a meal of sorts was about to be served.

We had not eaten for two days now, and for all my fear I knew it was incumbent on me to somehow advantage us of the situation. Imploring Nicolae and Elone to stay together where they were I crawled reptant to the very edge of the barrack floor to establish my prospects and realised my best hope lay in clambering into the room itself, there to take my chances when the men returned.

There was no time to consider the risks. An opportunity presented itself and I acted, propelling myself through the doorway as the last man hurried out, then rushing to a window to see if I had been observed.

I watched discreetly as the men collected their meagre rations from a makeshift canteen and in seconds ravenously consumed them, throwing their enamelware into a box before turning and heading back to where I waited.

I panicked, acutely aware my discovery was just seconds away. I looked about the hut in desperation then, as the door opened, I flung myself beneath a bed and trembled there, not daring to breathe, as the workers filed in silently. The Kapo barked an order in a language I did not recognise, turned and left. This was my first realisation that these men were not Germans but rather fellow internees of the camp, somehow elevated in rank above their peers.

Immediately the door closed the room erupted into whispered discussions in a multitude of languages and my heart leapt when I distinguished Romanian voices among them.

From my hiding place I could see the men were donning boots, preparing for their day's labour, but my mind concentrated on isolating the Romanian speakers from the others. By chance I realised one such native of my homeland was astride the bed only a metre or so from me and I moved my body quietly to a position where I could, at the chosen moment, attract his attention.

Suddenly the men were rising, boots tied, making for the door.

Throwing caution to the wind I seized my chance and in a loud whisper hissed, "Friend, please help me."

I held my breath as a dozen men turned, startled to hear a young girl's voice emanate from beneath a bunk in their midst.

I braved their incredulous stares and edged out from the bed, eyes pleading as I sought words to explain my plight. "Please, we need your help."

The Romanian speaker stared at me in disbelief, while other men, not cognizant of my language, shared sharp exchanges in their own. Finally, the man I had addressed found his voice.

"Child, what are you doing here? Do you wish to have us all killed? What is this madness?"

Emotion over-ruled caution and I clambered out from beneath the bunk and flung myself at him, placing myself at his mercy, tears streaming, struggling to be coherent.

"Please, we are starved and exhausted. We are looking for our mother. She was sent here from Medgidia to work. We have tracked her this far and now we –"

"Medgidia?" The voice came from behind me. "Anca?"

I stopped in mid-sentence at the sound of my name. The voice was familiar, but I could not place it in my confused mind. I turned to confront its owner and was met by a face that gazed upon mine with mutual disbelief.

He said again, "Anca? My God, Anca, is it you?"

I studied the face, the man, for long seconds, trying to draw some cognisance from the scrawny frame that spoke my name, for his skin was drawn tight like paper over bones that struggled to expose themselves to the day. His hair had receded, his eyes hollow, his back bent.

But still I recognized, from this travesty of a human being, the form of Maxim, father to my dear friend Raisa.

Chapter 59.

I flung myself upon his withered frame, almost sending him to the floor, screaming, "Maxim? Maxim? I cannot believe it is you!"

Then, as realisation dawned, "Raisa? What of Raisa? Is she here with you? Tell me she is well, Maxim. Please tell me she is well?"

It took all Maxim's strength to peel my body from his and bring me to arms length, hushing me urgently, anxious glances cast about him. He turned to his fellow Romanian and said quietly, "It is alright. She is no Nazi stooge. This is Anca Pasculata, daughter of Petre Bogdan, the Romanian resistance leader executed this year. I will deal with her. You go. Keep the Kapo occupied. I will join you as soon as I can."

There were further excited exchanges in different languages. Maxim addressed his fellows in Romanian, then Russian, then Polish. Someone else translated his words into a further language, possibly Magyar, and the men began to exit the barrack, casting nervous glances at me, before disappearing from view. As the last man left Maxim drew me to the window, where he could keep watch.

"Forgive me, Anca, if I am brusque and appear unfriendly. I mean you no harm, you know that, but if you are caught here then you and I, and a dozen others to set an example, will be stood before the Black Wall before this day is out. Now, quickly child, how did you get into our quarters?"

I tried to explain, but my words gushed and were incoherent. I wanted to know of Raisa, my best friend, and of Mama, of course, but my urgent tones made no sense to him.

I put my questions again, demanding he enlighten me. Of Raisa, was she well?

He said, "Anca, I was hoping it was you who would tell me. Did you not see her, in the women's quarters?"

His question was one of hope, for of course he supposed I had somehow just come from there, but I could only disappoint him.

"We have not been that far yet, Maxim. We..."

It was impossible to explain, and I suspect I would not have been believed had I attempted to do so.

"We have just arrived. Mama was sent here and we are looking for her." Then, "Maxim... Do you know if she is here?"

Maxim took my hands, offering physical comfort to substitute the bad news I realised he was to impart. I prepared myself.

"Anca, I have not seen your mother since before you left Medgidia. That is not to say she is not here. That she is not alive and well. There are thousands, perhaps tens of thousands, of prisoners here. But too there is death."

He hesitated, as if unwilling to continue.

"Typhus is rampant here, my child, though that would be a merciful release."

He stopped himself, looking into my eyes, then, "Death is all around us, Anca. I am sorry, but it would not be fair to raise your hopes."

I struggled to control my emotions, wanting, needing to know more.

"We have been here some three months now, Anca. We were dragged from our homes one night, not long after your own family were taken. Ours was a less dignified exit. Being of Russian descent the Nazis believed we would be troublesome, for rumour has it the Red Army is making much progress in the east. Why they could not kill us there and then and be done with us I do not know, but rather we were crammed into cattle trucks and transported into Poland."

I nodded to confirm I understood.

"I was sent to Treblinka first, but that has been closed now, torn down brick by brick as the Red Army advanced. Raisa and her mother were brought directly here to Auschwitz. I feared I would never see either of them again, but I glimpsed Raisa only a week or so ago, across a fence, so I can tell you she, at least, has survived so far."

My heart leapt at this news. "Oh Maxim, I am so relieved. I will find her. I promise you. But what of Catherine? Your wife? Raisa's mother?"

Maxim's eyes glazed, his voice stricken. "Anca, you will remember Catherine was lame of leg, crippled by polio from when she was herself a child."

I nodded, indifferent to this fact. Her infirmity had never prevented her being a fine mother to Raisa.

"They have no use for cripples here, Anca." Maxim clutched my hand and I watched a lone tear roll down his cheek. "She was taken to the showers on the first day, Anca. Somehow, for some reason, Raisa was spared, thank the Lord, but Catherine..."

He could contain himself no longer. Weak of body and spirit his emotions were released and he wept openly in my arms.

I persisted, "Maxim, you say she was taken to the showers? You make no sense to me."

Still crying he took my arms as if to provide support for me. "I do not begin to understand how you can have arrived here so ignorant, my child, but let me make this clear to you."

He looked directly at me. "The Nazis have no use for the elderly or infirm, Anca. Nor for the ailing or sick, nor for young children or the unskilled. Those who can work, who can make some contribution to the German war machine, are selected for their labour. I was lucky, Anca. I am a lapidary by trade, as you know, so I was plucked from the crowd to do their bidding. My skill is in the setting of precious stones. Even in war these barbarians still have the ability to appreciate beauty."

Maxim paused, searching for the right words to continue. "The rest, Anca... Those that had no skill or ability to offer, those too old or too young to be of use to them, were sent to the showers."

"The showers?" I looked at him in bewilderment, still not understanding.

Maxim grasped me tightly. "Anca, the showers do not spray water, they spray gas. Lethal gas."

I was shaking my head, no words forming, unwilling, unable, to believe what I was hearing.

Maxim clutched me to his skeletal chest and I flung my arms around his wasted body, touching protruding bone through translucent skin.

He said quietly, "This is not a labour camp, Anca. This is a death camp."

Chapter 60.

As we lay hidden beneath the barracks that day I was quite numb.

For all that Henryk had tried to warn me, for all I had seen, still Maxim's words occupied my every thought. It was all I could do to contain my emotions and stop my body trembling, but for the sake of Elone and Nicolae, huddled against me, I knew I had to keep control.

For all I had recently witnessed, sanity itself dictated it could not be true.

Birds sang and a blue sky could be faintly seen beyond the ashen smog, throwing my very memories into question.

Maxim must surely have been mistaken, I reasoned, for his tale of showers that issued forth gas instead of water was simply too incredible to believe. Catherine must have succumbed to typhus and her husband, wrought with ill-health, had allowed his imagination to conjure demonic acts even the Nazis were surely incapable of.

My warning to the children that we were to spend the day in hiding was ill-received and it was all I could do to keep Nicolae from crying out loud as fatigue and hunger combined to weaken his resistance. Elone too was becoming restless and I knew we would not manage a further day in these conditions without one or other of the children inadvertently exposing our plight.

Maintaining silence was perhaps the single most difficult of our myriad problems. On previous occasions I had been able to alleviate our suffering by resorting to light banter and song, but with Nazi jackboots passing us by only a few metres distant even whispered conversation was too great a risk to take.

Yet somehow, Elone perhaps sensing my fear, and Nicolae's frail body already succumbing to inanition, we managed to avoid detection and as dusk approached I began to prepare myself for the daunting task ahead.

The men returned from their work as darkness began to fall. Across the way the mobile canteen was wheeled out and for the second time that day our nostrils could enjoy the sensation of food our bodies could only hunger for.

But Maxim had not forsaken us.

As the men returned to enter their dwelling a crowd began to congregate by the door and a squabble broke out. At first I was alarmed by this development, fearing it would attract unwanted attention so close to our hiding place, but realised it was a deliberate artifice designed to cover Maxim's movements when suddenly a hand appeared beneath the hut pushing a canister of water and hunk of bread towards us. As I crawled forward to gratefully retrieve the offering I heard a Kapo advance on the squabbling men and bring them quickly to order with a crack of his whip. Seconds later the door was slammed shut and bolted and we were alone once more.

I divided the bread equally between Nicolae and Elone but partook of a few sips of water, fearing thirst might otherwise prove my downfall.

Elone protested briefly my abstinence then gave in to her own hunger and consumed her bread in a few quick mouthfuls.

If nutritionally deficient the meal had a powerful psychological effect, satisfying hunger and permitting both children to relax. Very soon they were both asleep, but I knew I could not join them, for fear of sleeping right through the long night and having to spend another day here.

If darkness was quickly upon us, the life of the camp seemed to continue for many hours more until eventually, as night became the early hours of morning, only the guards remained attentive, and these more to their own concerns than their duties.

I roused the children and we began again to trace our way across the camp, this time advantaged by the vague directions Maxim had set us.

It took us four long nights to traverse Auschwitz, such was the scale of the camp, for entire factories occupied this vast site, producing everything from cloth to military hardware.

If Maxim's words had reinforced the concerns Henryk had expressed, the enormity of Auschwitz had still to filter through to a young mind incapable of imagining the truth.

.But any residual doubt, any hiding behind the hope of exaggeration or misinformation, was to be dispelled on our fourth day beneath the barracks, on our way to the women's quarters.

Chapter 61.

We had, all three of us, fallen asleep in our latest shelter when we were startled to hear the whistle of a locomotive in the distance. In the dark of the night there had been no opportunity to study our latest view, but the locomotive's piercing scream introduced us to a new day and with it new terrors.

Somehow Nicolae was energised by the steam engine's approach, awakening the boy within that enfeebled skeleton of a child that had for the past three days followed me like a mindless automaton from one hiding place to the next. Clinging, never letting go, of Elone's hand.

Yet now he was aware once more, eyes almost bright, eager to see the train approach. So thrilled was I by this ostensive recovery that I abandoned caution and allowed all three of us to advance as far forward as we dared, to purchase a view.

It was evident now we had found the far perimeter of the site, all but adjacent to the glowing chimneys we had spied on our arrival, and as we watched two huge gates were opened across a railway siding that entered the camp just a few hundred metres distant. As the train crossed the perimeter boundary music, Wagner I would later learn, began broadcasting from loudspeakers hung liberally around the concourse where Nazi guards, Kapos and labourers waited to greet the new arrivals.

The locomotive ground to a halt, dragging the ophidian cattle trucks shuddering in its wake and I saw Nicolae's expression change as memories of our own tragic journey were rekindled in his mind. I wanted to draw him back, to shield him, but he held tight to Elone's hand. I wanted to pull him to me, but instead we watched, silently mesmerized by the scene of ostensive welcome.

As the doors were opened and the passengers began to tumble out we were relieved to see them mostly fit and able, if exhausted from their journey, which I surmised must have been of much shorter duration than our own terrifying ride to have allowed them to keep so well.

The first wagons carried women and children, the latter men, though none wore the distinguishing brassard pronouncing them to be Jews.

As we watched, families join together on the concourse after their journey, children and wives hurrying to their fathers and husbands. I was filled with envy, the fear instilled by Henryk's and Maxim's words evaporating as the sound of joyous families reunited raised even above the loud music.

It was obvious enough to me now that Maxim was mistaken, misled somehow by rumour and innuendo, his mind weakened by poor health, mistaking the fatalities caused by typhus for the work of the Nazis, and I felt my spirits rise.

The music stopped and Nazi guards stepped forward, addressing hundreds of people in broken Polish, confirming my suspicion that these were local people, having been brought from within Poland to work.

Someone asked, "Where is our luggage?" and for a brief few seconds my worst fears danced across my mind as I realised not a single valise accompanied them, bringing back vivid memories of the scene I had witnessed in Warsaw. A guard assured them their trunks were in the end wagon and would be unloaded shortly, and somehow I allowed myself to believe it, for in doing so I gained hope we would soon find our mother.

The guards began to move among the new arrivals, asking them their trades and skills, directing those with valued abilities to a separate area, requesting the others remain where they were. My pulse quickened as I heard a woman respond she was a seamstress and watched with keen interest as she was directed to stand with the select few. This was Mama's trade and evidently a valued one. Most surely had she arrived safely at Auschwitz she would have been selected for her skills and might even now be employed somewhere close by.

As I watched the segregation of skilled and unskilled workers continue my hopes rose still further and I found myself clutching the hands of Elone and Nicolae, a faint smile playing on my lips.

Quite soon the separation was complete and the skilled workers were led away, assured they would meet their families again later, once they had been fully assessed.

Then the Nazi guard turned on the several hundred Poles still standing on the concourse and warned them that the camp was rife with typhus, a fatal disease transmitted by lice, and that for this reason all new arrivals had to be disinfected before entry into the camp could be permitted. Why the selected skilled workers should have been taken through without this precaution was not explained.

I watched the crowd directed to some windowless barracks just a short way distant, following a path which ran by our hideaway.

My mind raced. This was our chance to join them, to sneak in amongst them as they passed, to go on to the cleansing showers, and to emerge refreshed and lice-free.

A smile played on my lips and I reached out to Nicolae's shoulder. From the showers we would surely be taken directly to the women's quarters, perhaps to find Mama that very day. It was all I could do not to rush out and announce ourselves.

As I edged forward, whispering to the children to make ready, I felt Elone touch my arm and looking to her could see alarm in her eyes.

As if reading my mind she whispered, "No, Anca, I do not like it. There is something wrong here."

Be it intuition or childlike fear, her prescience concerned me, for I could not banish entirely from my mind the words of Maxim. If his crazed denunciation of the showers was just too incredible to be believed, still his tortured features haunted my mind, warning me all was not as it seemed.

I took a deep breath, closing my eyes, searching for the correct response. The right decision. At last I said quietly, "You are right, Elone. Now is not the time."

Chapter 62.

We watched in silent fascination as the hundreds of people were led to the windowless barracks, there to be made to strip naked on the concourse, men, women and children alike, old and young together, evidently indifferent to their nudity, perhaps accepting it was the price they paid for their future security. I thought fleetingly of the scene on the hill I had witnessed from Henryk's truck. But this was different, I told myself. The showers were right alongside.

A patina of frost still clung to the hard ground and a cold wind blew through the camp, making the would-be bathers shiver and hold their arms about themselves to keep warm.

Guided by Kapos, labourers began to gather their clothes, throwing the garments onto carts. To be disinfected, the curious were told.

More men appeared, carrying large sheets which they lay on the ground then, as we watched, these naked people were made to stand astride and their body hair, from their heads, beneath their arms, everywhere, was shaven clean. To prevent the typhus lice breeding I heard the Kapos explain.

Only when every person, adult and child alike, had been so treated, were they led to the showers. How many were crammed into each room I could not tell, but somehow every person there was found a place in one or other of the buildings and the doors closed around them.

The sheets of hair were carefully gathered and carted away, to what end I could not begin to guess.

Now the concourse was all but empty, only a few guards remaining, indifferent to the Poles awaiting their fumigation within.

Nothing more to see, we eased our way back to our secure hiding place beneath the hut and huddled together for warmth. I stroked Elone's hair, thankful we had not presented ourselves as I had considered, a smile playing on my lips to imagine her head shaven.

But my smile was short lived as the first screams began.

Bewildered, we stared about us, perplexed as to where the sound emanated, but in seconds it was obvious. Maxim's words came flooding back to me, of the fate met by his wife Catherine, taken to the shower rooms on her first day.

As the screams became louder I hugged Nicolae to me, futilely covering his ears with my hands.

Elone was clutching me, her eyes wide with fear, streaming tears, looking to me for salvation, but I could offer none.

For perhaps twenty minutes the screams continued unabated, tortured screams of men, women and children, enduring a fate I could not begin to imagine.

And then the screams began to subside and minutes later there was only silence, broken by the incessant, uncontrollable sobbing of three terrified children, alone and afraid in the very heart of Auschwitz-Birkenau.

Chapter 63.

Nicolae was in shock, a low whine barely audible, that I could no nothing to quell, and I feared Elone would soon join him.

We clung together, lost innocents in this place of darkness and malificence. Yet somehow, for all I had seen and heard, my mind could not embrace the truth.

For all I had witnessed... My father's execution; the brutal murder on the platform in Bucharest; the mowing down of lines of Jews outside Plaszow; the screams that still echoed loudly in my mind... For all Henryk and Maxim had warned me, still I could not conceive of the enormity... Of the sheer scale of the extermination taking place here.

It was so unreal that I began telling myself it had not happened. That hunger and fatigue had produced some horrific collective hallucination between us. That I would shortly wake up in a warm bed at home and find the whole thing had been no more than an obscene nightmare.

I wanted to comfort the children, to deny what they had heard, to give them hope, but my brain had all but ceased to control my body. I found myself being drawn back to the edge of the hut despite myself, not wanting, but needing, to see. To assure myself it had not taken place, that I was somehow mistaken.

For a moment, perhaps minutes, perhaps an hour, it was as if nothing had happened. The concourse was deserted, the shower rooms silent. A cool autumn sun was breaking through the smog of ash that drifted incessantly from the furnace chimneys now just a short way distant. From afar I could hear the sounds of industry as the factories churned out their deadly munitions.

Closer still I heard voices, human voices, from within the shower barracks and I was craning myself forward, desperate to believe, willing those hundreds of naked Poles to walk back out into the cold day, cleansed and disinfected, ready to don clean clothes and take up their duties.

As the doors opened from within it was all I could do to contain my joy and rush out to greet them. To embrace them. To celebrate their very existence.

But the dream turned to macabre reality as the first labourer appeared in his striped prison uniform, dragging a cart behind him. If I knew what was on the cart even before it emerged into view, still I looked, unable to tear my eyes from this grisly scene.

I watched, unwillingly, unable to turn away, as cartloads of tangled bodies were drawn across the concourse before me, quietly borne to the furnaces in the distance.

And as I watched the true nature of these ovens became apparent. These four huge chimneys rising above the birch trees represented no industrial process but one. They were crematoria, designed and built for the sole purpose to dispose of the bodies of the innocent victims of Auschwitz-Birkenau.

Chapter 64.

Even to this day I do not quite know how we survived the months that followed.

We were without food, our thirst quenched only by the rain that shortly began to fall, turning the hard ground of autumn into a quagmire of mud and slime. Only when the mud became so deep that it penetrated beneath the hut to our hiding place could I muster the will to go on, to move elsewhere.

If I had not yet abandoned all hope of finding Mama, buoyed by the possibility that her skills as a seamstress may have proved her salvation, still my first concern was to protect Nicolae and Elone from this dread necropolis.

We moved by night, like mindless automatons, gaining advantage from the inclement weather that saw the guards sheltering from the cold rain. If the electrified perimeter fences with their barbed wire and watchtowers were carefully avoided, still we managed to wander about the site with relative impunity.

Eventually we were driven from our hiding places by the flood of mud and filth accumulating, and were forced to seek shelter in unlocked buildings.

One such place we found ourselves in proved our salvation, yet ironically was the very centre of the death industry that was the purpose of Auschwitz-Birkenau.

We were there for many weeks, perhaps months, I cannot be sure, hiding behind hundreds of cans marked with the legend Zyklon B. If I had realised then these canisters contained hydrogen cyanide, the very gas used to exterminate tens, perhaps hundreds of thousands of innocent people, surely we would have moved on. But it was warm and dry, and in truth perhaps we would have sheltered there regardless, for our very survival depended on it.

From the security of this improbable refuge I foraged by night for food, collecting discarded crusts of bread or half-eaten tins of salted beef thrown down by the Nazi guards, scavenging like a wild animal. This combination of meagre rations and the dry warmth that permitted us to rest peacefully bar our dreams, meant that slowly, so very slowly, we began to regain our strength and Nicolae and Elone to emerge from their cocoon of shock.

If at first our only thoughts were to stay alive, as the days passed and we remained undisturbed we became increasingly confident. Our lassitude was lifting with each small meal, and each day we remained undiscovered I foraged further afield, sometimes brazenly approaching Nazi barracks, listening at windows in the hope I would hear a language I understood, or find food or information that would assist our campaign of survival.

I even managed to clothe us, when I stumbled upon a row of huts each laden with garments of all purpose and size.

At first I thought I had found the warehouses for the clothes manufactured on site, but I was quickly disabused of this idea when I dragged a coat to the light and saw the Jewish brassard upon the sleeve. Yet by now I was beyond shock.

As I rifled through coats, dresses and underwear selecting items that might fit us, as I clambered over a huge pile of thousands, literally thousands, of children's shoes looking for a pair to fit my little brother's feet, I knew well their origins. But by now I was indifferent, perhaps even beyond caring, that these were all that remained of innocent children brought here with their parents to work, only to be slaughtered like so many cattle.

All that now mattered was our own survival: Nicolae's, Elone's and mine.

I drew hope from the increasing laxity of the guards within the compounds, where they seemed to wander aimlessly about, indifferent to their duties. Occasionally I would hear snippets of information in Polish and with it began to gather hope. Rumour told of the Red Army's approach and I was aware the atmosphere of the camp had changed.

Chapter 65.

Perhaps the first tangible evidence was when the ashen smog of cremated bodies began to dissipate and fresh, winter air began to penetrate our lungs.

Slowly the skies cleared and we could see the clouds once more.

Then the demolition began, at first orderly, later with more urgency, with less attention to detail. I watched the crematoria chimneys slowly pulled down, each night when I ventured out witnessing some advance in their destruction, and for the first time began to hope again.

I had by now lost all track of time, only the seasonal changes providing an amorphous calendar within my confused mind, but I knew autumn had passed and winter was well advanced. Snow was particularly unwelcome, not so much for the cold, for that we had come to accept, but because I feared tell-tale footprints left behind might announce our presence.

So long had we been here in this makeshift domicile, resident among these pernicious canisters, ensconced amid oddments of clothing for comfort and warmth, subsisting on the dregs raided from Nazi rubbish bins, that we began to feel at home, daring to believe we could survive the winter here, perhaps even the duration of the war.

But such complacency proved misplaced.

It was early morning, a cold sun's watery rays illuminating another freezing day. We were huddled together for warmth, the three of us, beneath a pile of coats and camisoles, when we heard their arrival. I was upright in an instant, fear dictating my actions, a hand each over Nicolae's and Elone's mouths to prevent them making a sound. Wide eyed they sat up, terror etched in their faces as we heard the Zyklon B canisters being loaded onto carts.

A small window to the rear of us provided the store's only light and surreptitiously prising it open I eased first Nicolae, then Elone, through the tiny gap. Even their small, emaciated bodies struggled to squeeze through and I feared for my own chances.

Both children were by now safely outside but as I clambered onto the ledge and began to prise myself through the tiny orifice my worst fears were realised. I became suspended halfway, my coat entangled with the window hook, leaving me hanging from the wall a half metre from the ground.

"Anca! Anca!" It was too much for my little brother and he cried out for me to join them, all caution forgotten at the sight of his sister struggling to free herself.

Too late, Elone grabbed him, urging him to be silent.

I heard angry shouts in guttural German and the sound of canisters being thrown to one side as a Nazi guard advanced on me from behind.

A heavy hand clasped my shoulders and I screamed out, "Nicolae! Elone! Run! Run!" I struggled violently as a thickset arm came around my neck and began dragging me back into the store. Limbs flailing, I lashed out as best I could, but to no avail, only the very size of the window's aperture preventing me being pulled back the way I had tried to leave. I could see my brother below me, watching helplessly, terrified, and was reminded it was not just my own fate that would be sealed were I to lose this battle.

Suddenly my tormentor's arm slipped over my chin and across my face and I seized my chance, biting deep into his wrist with an animal-like ferocity born of desperation.

With a scream of pain his arm was gone and I fell back to my halfway position, hung pendent by my coat. Angry voices shouted at the window even as Elone pushed her tiny body beneath mine, taking my weight, allowing me the leverage I needed to slip my arms from the coat sleeves. I fell to the cold ground, free, leaving the garment dangling from the window.

I grabbed the children, one under each arm, and with a celerity that surprised us all managed to carry both my charges across the concourse to the shelter of another building. Even as we cornered the hut, a spray of gunfire spattered the ground behind us.

We stopped for breath, to get our bearings, fearing the worst, but from our tormentor all we heard was a cold laugh, as if somehow he found amusement at our determination. He shouted out across the concourse, though I recognized only the word Kinder, children, and hoped our escapade had been dismissed as a harmless child's prank.

Chapter 66.

A punishing hoarfrost had descended overnight, rendering the ground gelid, our return to hiding beneath barracks buildings all the more difficult after our relative comfort in the store-room. I knew we would not survive many nights so exposed, and was slowly realising that, for better or worse, we must soon present ourselves and accept our fate.

If the showers of death had been abandoned and destroyed, as I knew they had, and the crematoria dismantled, then it was just possible a more tolerant regime now ruled Auschwitz, that would permit us the singular luxury of continued life.

We huddled together and shivered the day away, and when night came Nicolae clung to Elone and I both, unwilling to let me leave them even to scavenge for food.

A second day passed.

A third.

Temperatures plummeted each night, barely rising to freezing point during the day. I studied the emaciated faces of Nicolae and Elone as night fell for the fourth time and knew that, when day next broke, I would have no alternative but to present all three of us to the mercy of the Nazi's cruel administration.

Those next few hours might prove our last, but I was determined we would confront our destiny with dignity and, if were soon to die, would do so as human beings, not animals.

As the dawn's early light I gathered the children to my breast, kissed each one and said quietly, "Come with me, little ones, and be brave. I cannot promise you a future, but we will surely die here before another night passes. Whatever happens, remember always I love you both."

I kissed them both. "But now, we are going to try find our Mama."

Chapter 67.

We emerged from our dark hiding place into the cold light of winter's day, our bodies tremulous in the sub-zero temperature. I clutched Nicolae and Elone to me, determined that, if our lives were soon to end we would at least die in one another's arms.

But we were greeted only by silence. An eerie, indifferent silence that neither gave hope, nor inspired fear.

There was no guard at the gate to the next compound and we walked cautiously towards it, expecting at any minute to feel the muzzle of a gun, the salivating teeth of a guard's vicious hound, or a bullet in the back.

But nothing happened.

We stopped at the gate, peering through, ready to throw ourselves at the mercy of the guard, but there was no-one, no-one at all, to greet us. I hesitated.

Frightened.

Bewildered.

This was not the scenario I had prepared myself for.

I felt Nicolae tug weakly at my hand, reminding me we must find food soon or perish regardless, and I knew we had to risk going on.

I pushed the gate open slowly, psyching myself for the inevitable confrontation, but none came. No guard rushed to threaten us, nor a spray of bullets to ward us off. Instinctively I looked to the watchtower, but could see no-one. I dismissed the observation, thinking it too distant to offer clarity.

Even so we became emboldened by our progress and proceeded cautiously across the concourse, towards the factory. Too weak to fend for ourselves any longer I knew we must present ourselves, beg for mercy and hope to be dealt with painlessly.

The factory was silent, and we were aware of a tangible aura of dereliction.

It was a relief then, but no surprise, to push open the doors and find nothing but abandoned machinery. I called out, daring there to be someone, but only the echo of my voice responded.

"Anca, where is everyone? What has happened?"

I turned to my sister, holding her close. "I do not know, Elone. We must investigate further."

We departed the factory, walking brazenly across the concourse, willing someone to challenge us, but still there was silence.

A lonely, palpable silence that haunted our every step.

For perhaps an hour or more we wandered between empty barracks, opening doors to deserted buildings, confronting non-existent guards, before we finally saw a figure, sitting propped against a wall in the distance.

I called out, but there was no response and we rushed across to him, hoping for explanation. But as we arrived at his side I recoiled in horror, shielding the children from the scene. For all the destruction I had witnessed recently, still I was not indifferent to death, and the sight of this skeletal corpse sickened me. But I could not help but study it.

A crystallised frosting disguised his features but there was no obvious sign of wounding and I could not help but wonder if it were cold or hunger that had smote his last breath where he sat.

I drew the children away and we began to hurry across the empty grounds, searching for the living in this desolate place of death.

We stumbled by accident upon a canteen and began searching among the abandoned pots and pans for any scrap of food that might be there. We were lucky to unearth a few cans of tinned meat from which we fed ourselves ravenously, without regard to etiquette or future needs, until all was gone. Thus nourished and fortified, we continued our search.

As we accosted further bodies I began to despair that we were the very last people alive in this evil place, but as we rounded a corner and entered a new compound we were elated to see a hundred or more people before us.

We shouted out, all of us, but barely a head turned, only indifference greeting us, and as we closed in on these people, adults and children, male and female alike, these skeletal frames burdened with despondency, my elation became fear. For these were people moribund, for whom the very will to live had been driven from their souls.

As we entered among them it became apparent many had already succumbed, some dead, other dying, literally before our eyes, where they lay on the frost-smitten ground.

I rushed among them, asking questions, trying to find answers, but was met by glazed indifference. Perhaps they did not understand me. More likely they were simply beyond caring. We began to move among them, looking for any fit enough to respond, but met only apathy, perhaps even resentment that we should intrude upon their last hours in this way.

I scanned the hopelessly attenuated bodies as we meandered between them, daring still to hope I might see Mama among these survivors.

We eventually came to the perimeter fence and I could confirm now that the watchtowers had been long abandoned, but still the forbidding barbed wire fences presented an impenetrable barrier to the outside world.

We turned back, once again stepping among the barely living, over the dead, the three of us hand in hand, snakelike across the yard, when I heard a feeble voice cry out.

"Anca? Anca? Tell me it is really you!"

My heart leapt, hoping this pitiful voice was my mother's, but as I descried the skeletal frame that addressed me, struggling to raise her head above a weakened body, I saw it was but a child of about my own age.

"Anca! It is you!"

I looked again, peering into those withdrawn eyes, trying to put a name to the frost-smitten features beneath shorn hair.

Then, emotion choking my voice, "Raisa!"

Chapter 68.

I was beside her in an instant, cradling her head against my side, pouring out incomprehensible questions amid a mixture of tears and sorrow, for if to meet again my best friend was a delight, to see her like this, moribund, resigned to die where she lay, was a pitiful sight I shall never strike from my mind.

Nicolae belatedly recognized Raisa and knelt beside us, taking her hand. Elone joined us, cognisant of the bond though she knew not the person.

If weak of body and spirit, our chance encounter seemed to invigorate Raisa and we managed to talk a while, sat on the cold ground, until she again began to show fatigue.

Weak as she was, Raisa managed to offer some explanation of events. The Red Army was advancing and the Nazis had abandoned the camp as I had surmised, destroying what they could, taking many thousands of able workers with them, heading west, on a long, tortuous journey by foot to camps nearer the German border. Those too weak or ill to travel, too old or too young, were simply left here at Auschwitz.

Left to die.

She asked of her father, Maxim. I was able to tell her I had seen him alive not long ago and how he had assisted us, and her features brightened. Knowing that her own mother had perished here in Auschwitz I could not bring myself to ask if Raisa knew Mama's fate.

I remembered the canteen we had encountered earlier and, promising we would return with sustenance, we rose to search for any remnant of food we might have first missed. Raisa's hand lingered in mine, unwilling to relinquish her grip, sunken eyes imploring me to stay, but I knew without food she would not survive the night.

Tearfully we made our way back, ambulate amid the dead and dying, to where we had earlier found our meal.

All around me people were starving, but I thought only of Raisa.

We found a single tin of beef, undoubtedly the last. There would be no more.

I held the tin in my hand, looking first at Nicolae, then at Elone, then thinking of Raisa, so close to death.

Elone took my hand. "Raisa must have it, Anca. Something will turn up for us, you will see."

I said, "You three will have it. You, Nicolae and Raisa."

Elone did not reply, but took Nicolae by the hand and began leading him back the way we had come. I quickly opened the tin and followed them, hiding the food in my pocket for fear of taunting the many starving people we would have to pass by to get to my friend.

By the time we returned to her darkness was once again encroaching, the temperature falling rapidly. I divided the contents of the can and gave a third each to Nicolae, Elone and Raisa. Elone immediately divided her share in half and gave a portion each to Nicolae and Raisa.

I could not find the words to express myself, simply hugging her to me as my brother and my friend gratefully ate.

Too weak to move of her own accord, it would have been impossible for us to carry Raisa between the dead and dying all around us, and I knew we must stay the night with her, out in the open, to shield her with our own bodies, for she would not survive another night unprotected.

We huddled together around her, Raisa's head on my lap, shivering as darkness closed in on us. At some stage I abandoned principle and took clothes from the dead around us to provide us with warmth, but still the cold penetrated deep.

Somehow Nicolae managed to find sleep, and later Raisa too. Elone stayed awake with me through the night, her indomitable spirit all that prevented me succumbing to the cold.

We talked of times past and times future, avoiding always the subject of the fate of our families. We spoke of what we would do when the war ended, where we might live, who we might marry. If the talk was aimless and futile still it kept us awake, the better to shield our slumbering partners.

But eventually I surrendered to sleep myself, waking again as dawn broke.

As the light of day began again to illuminate our wretched surroundings desolation loomed large. Still more bodies littered the concourse, still fewer managed to stand or even sit up.

Elone held my hand tight, and as I studied her face in the crepuscular light I could see tears in her eyes. I became alarmed, unsure of her concern.

"Elone, what is it?"

She did not look up, but said quietly, "I am sorry, Anca. Your friend has gone."

It took a few seconds for the meaning of her words to penetrate my mind before I fell upon Raisa's body and wept. Elone comforted Nicolae while I clutched Raisa's lifeless form to my breast until emotion finally succumbed to reality and I conceded defeat.

She had been my best friend, but now she was no more.

Still I had Nicolae and Elone, of course, but for now I could only think of Raisa.

Elone retrieved the amulet from around her neck and passed it to me, no words necessary.

I took it gratefully and placed it over Raisa's still head, before pulling her coat over her.

I began to cry again.

Chapter 69.

Just hours later the first soldier arrived, the advance guard of the Russian Red Army, to announce our liberation.

It was January twenty-seventh, nineteen forty-five, and for us the war was over.

But for my dear friend Raisa, and for countless hundreds of thousands of innocents like her, they arrived too late.

Chapter 70.

"Mrs. Jones, are you okay?"

I felt a comforting hand on my shoulder as Mr. Wilkinson's concerned voice intruded on my thoughts.

I looked around me and the distraught faces of Nicolae and Elone, the children of Auschwitz-Birkenau, became the distraught faces of Class 9B.

Through my tears the pediculous garments of that dread necropolis faded, to be replaced by pristine school skirt and trousers, shirt and blouse.

I struggled for words, but none would come.

In all these decades since that day I had never had cause or desire to tell my story, at first unable, later believing no-one would wish to hear it.

Now, as I looked around to see these school students in tears with me, children made oblivious to the reality of man's inhumanity to man by the fantasy of television and film, I felt pangs of guilt that I had ripped apart their innocence, burdening them with knowledge of events past that many would argue were best left forgotten.

A child from the front row came forward with a tissue and I took it gratefully. I felt her hand slip into mine and as I looked at her I could see Raisa's face staring back at me.

I dabbed my eyes and Raisa was gone, replaced by this caring schoolgirl, gripping my rugose fingers, comforting me.

She asked, "What of your mother, Anca? Tell us, did you find her?"

Mr. Wilkinson stepped forward. "No more questions, Jennifer."

He turned to me. "Mrs. Jones, there's no need to say any more. If you wish to leave now we quite understand."

I gestured for him to let me continue. "Thank you, but they have a right to know."

I turned to the class, dabbing my eyes, struggling to control my voice.

"Would that this were just a story, a fairy-tale, for then perhaps I could offer you a happy ending." I looked about them, every pair of eyes upon me. "But the Holocaust was no fairy-tale. There was no happy ending."

I paused, myriad emotions straining to be unleashed, but somehow I kept control.

"No, Jennifer, I never saw my mother again. Almost certainly she was taken to Auschwitz. No less certainly she died there, though I will never know for sure, and in truth it is the not knowing that hurts the most."

I sensed they wished to hear more.

"Elone's parents, Chaim and Golda, both perished. We later learned that Golda had died on the train journey to Auschwitz, even before the derailment that liberated the children and I. Chaim, on a different train, probably the same one that carried my mother, arrived at Auschwitz expecting to be reunited with his wife and daughter."

I struggled with the words. "He was a Jew with no special skills and in poor health. He was sent directly to the showers on arrival."

Ben, the boy who had been so indifferent to my story when I had begun, put up a hand tentatively. He asked, "What of Maxim, Raisa's father?"

I tried to smile at Ben, to acknowledge the thoughtfulness of his question. "He was taken away on the Long March, for his lapidary skills were valued. Given his parlous health it is unlikely he completed the journey."

I saw Ben choke back tears.

"Maxim's daughter, my dear friend Raisa, was buried by the Russians in a communal grave close to Auschwitz. One anonymous body among tens of thousands. But at least she was given the dignity of a grave. Most of the millions of victims of the Nazi Holocaust were denied even that."

The room was silent, glazed eyes imploring me to continue.

"Of course, there were survivors, myself among them. Nicolae, Elone and I are still alive today to challenge those who say the Holocaust never happened, although Nicolae was thankfully too young to remember much of it."

Ben asked, "Do you still see one another?"

I smiled. "Elone, even now, I still think of as my sister. She was a remarkable child who grew up to be a remarkable woman. For all her suffering she was able to distinguish the Nazi from the German, and later married a German man. She lives to this day in Berlin. We keep in contact still, but there are some things we never talk about. Some things are too painful... Even now, after all this time..."

I began to cry again and Mr. Wilkinson attended me, helping me to my feet. "Mrs. Jones, I think you have told us enough. Perhaps you'd like a cup of tea. I'll escort you to the staff-room."

As he walked me past the seated children sombre, glistening eyes stared up at me, gentle hands reaching out to offer comfort. I knew I could never go through this again, to relive those terrible memories a further time.

Perhaps I should never have come here today.

But as I felt Ben's hand in mine, clutching tightly at my fingers, I realised that, if even one child there went from that class believing, determined, that those tragic events we call the Holocaust should never be allowed to happen again, then the innocent victims of the Nazis had not died wholly in vain.

Chapter 71.

I sat in the staff room, refreshed by a cup of sweet tea.

Mr. Wilkinson, having assured me that my talk had had a profound impact on his pupils, had gone to his next class, leaving me alone with my thoughts.

A television was on low in the background, a twenty-four hour rolling news channel, and suddenly I was crying again. This time not over events many decades past, but over tragedies taking place even now.

As I watched reports of ethnic cleansing, of terrorism and genocide, still taking place around the globe today, I could not help but wonder if we had learned anything at all.

END

29940130R00136

Made in the USA
Lexington, KY
12 February 2014